MATCHING THE MARQUESS

MARRYWELL BRIDES
BOOK THREE

DARCY BURKE

Zealous Quill Press

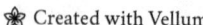

For Luna Kitten, the sweetest, snuggliest cat who steals my chair and yells at me if I stop petting her.

MATCHING THE MARQUESS

Benjamin Nash, Marquess of Creslow, must marry, for he is the last of the family line. Desirous of a business arrangement instead of a love match, he hires a matchmaker, only to learn she's the widow he nearly seduced during a house party. Though attraction still simmers between them, he agrees to keep their relationship professional.

After the death of her philandering husband left her a pauper, Rebecca Sweet finds financial hope as a matchmaker. Engaged with her first real client, she's stymied by his requirement that love is not allowed—and by the fact that she can't stop thinking of his kisses.

But when they seek to find his bride at her hometown's matchmaking festival, she must face the guilt of her past. The marquess's surprising support makes her wonder if she could take a second chance on love. Too bad he's only interested in a casual affair. She needs to find him a bride before she loses her heart forever.

Don't miss any of **Marrywell Brides**!

Love romance? Have a free book (or two or three) on me!

Sign up at http://www.darcyburke.com/join for members-only exclusives, including advance notice of pre-orders and insider scoop, as well as contests, giveaways, freebies, and 99 cent deals!

Want to share your love of my books with like-minded readers? Want to hang with me and get inside scoop? Then don't miss my exclusive Facebook groups!

Darcy's Duchesses for historical readers
Burke's Book Lovers for contemporary readers

CHAPTER 1

Leighton Buzzard, September, 1817

*R*ebecca Sweet had never attended a house party before, let alone one hosted by a baron and baroness. Her life for the past nine years had been that of a simple country wife and then widow of a modest farmer who spent more than he earned and took his ease drinking ale and gambling with friends or finding comfort in his mistress's arms. This sort of event with planned entertainments and servants seeing to Rebecca's needs was far beyond her experience.

But things had changed for her in the eight months since her husband's death. His Aunt Jennet, a country gentlewoman, whose dearest friend just happened to be a baroness, had taken Rebecca in. Now, Rebecca was reaping the rewards of their association, even if she felt a trifle awkward doing so. She just wasn't sure where she belonged. Her husband's house hadn't ever felt like home, and Aunt Jennet's house didn't either. Rebecca thought back to her childhood, to Black Sheep Farm in Marrywell, but that hadn't felt like a home either.

Could a sprawling house such as Clipstone Hedge, where she was now, with its red brick and golden stone exterior and too many rooms to count, feel like a home? Perhaps, but it depended on the people inside it. Rebecca realized it was up to her to make a home for herself. She just wasn't sure how that would happen.

What she could do, however, was perhaps repay Aunt Jennet's kindness. Her granddaughter, Delia, was also in attendance, and Rebecca had noted that she and a young gentleman at the party seemed to share an affinity for several things. Rebecca was fairly certain they might develop an attachment, but both were shy and might need a little assistance. Earlier, Rebecca had suggested they play chess since they both said they enjoyed it.

They'd played and seemed to have a wonderful time together, as far as Rebecca could tell from her position across the drawing room. With a little more help, they might indeed make a match. The thought filled Rebecca with delight, and not just because it would please Aunt Jennet. Watching two people fall in love was perhaps the closest Rebecca would get to doing so herself. She would take all the joy she could from that.

Rebecca moved farther into the library. With its towering shelves crammed with books and multiple cozy seating areas, it nearly overwhelmed her. Books represented wealth, and this was a display almost beyond her imagination.

She ought to be asleep as it was nearly two in the morning, but lulling herself into a restful state, especially in a place that wasn't her home, had always been a challenge. She'd thought a book might help, but wasn't sure how to find something that interested her.

Walking near the bookcases, she gently trailed her fingertips along the spines. Randomly, she chose one and flipped open the cover. *Sheep and Goats: The Intricacies of Animal Husbandry*. That sounded…dry. She moved to another shelf and removed another tome. *Robinson Crusoe*. Much better. She'd already read that, but perhaps she'd find another novel that she hadn't.

After a few minutes of perusing, she found a copy of *Pamela* by Samuel Richardson. It looked impossibly long. Not that she could finish any of these books before leaving tomorrow, for she was much too slow a reader.

"Good evening."

Rebecca startled at the sound of the man's voice and dropped the book on her toe. She gasped and pulled her foot from under the heavy tome.

"My apologies!" The gentleman rushed forward. He bent to retrieve the book from the floor just as she did the same.

His fingers met hers upon the leather cover. Then their gazes clashed.

Rebecca's heart vaulted into her throat. She recognized him, for he'd only arrived late that afternoon. The hostess, Lady Philpott, was his cousin, and he was the Marquess of Creslow.

A. Bloody. Marquess.

He was breathtakingly handsome, with thick, dark coffee-colored hair, a wide forehead, expressive brows, a patrician nose with a fascinating dimple at the end, lips that were perhaps a touch too wide for a man, and a sculpted jaw and chin that looked as if it belonged on one of the statues in the garden behind the assembly rooms in Marrywell, where she'd grown up. And now that she was this close to him, she could see his eyes were a warm chestnut brown with a smattering of gold flecks near the center. She could very well lose herself in his stare...

"Shall I remove my hand?" he asked softly, almost teasingly.

"Unless you were hoping to read this novel?" She presumed he'd come to the library for the same reason she had. They were both wearing night-clothes. She'd donned a thick dressing gown over her night rail, and he sported a dark green velvet banyan over his pantaloons, which encased his muscular legs.

Overall, he presented an image of unrelenting masculinity that had the effect of somehow making her feel more feminine. Or perhaps more aware of her femininity. She struggled not to fix on the tri-angle of light sandstone-hued flesh exposed at the base of his throat.

"What's the title?" he asked. "Perhaps it may suit."

"*Pamela.*"

His brows rose. "A provocative choice." Their hands were still touching, and the word *provocative* only made Rebecca more aware of the connection. "You've read it before?"

She shook her head. His lips spread in an alluring smile, and Rebecca's breath arrested in her lungs.

He took his hand away. "I shan't deprive you of it."

Rebecca tamped down her disappointment at the loss of his touch, but then he clasped her elbow and helped her to stand. She didn't need his assistance, but found it more than pleasant.

"You've read it?" she asked.

"Yes." He released her arm, and she suffered an-other twinge of disappointment. "We passed a copy around at Eton—under the noses of our masters, mind you. They would not have approved."

"Why not?"

"It's the story of a young maid who is seduced—in reality, she is abused—by her employer."

"That doesn't sound like anything I would want to read."

"It's strangely compelling, but I actually found it…" He grimaced. "I don't wish to spoil it any further for you."

She held the book to her chest. "Don't concern yourself with that. It's not as if I'll be able to finish it tonight, and the party concludes tomorrow."

"You could just take it with you." He leaned slightly toward her. His scent of sandalwood and something indescribably male enveloped her in sensation. Why did a scent make her want to move closer to him?

"Are you suggesting I steal it?" she whispered.

He lifted a shoulder. "I presume you'd return it. Unless you live very far away?"

Did he not remember that she resided with Lady Philpott's dearest friend just a short distance from Clipstone Hedge? "I suppose I *could* borrow it."

"I think you should. Just look at their library." He glanced about. "My cousin and her husband won't miss it."

"Is that what you planned to do?" Rebecca asked. "Select a book and take it with you when you leave tomorrow?"

He laughed. "In fact, I am staying tomorrow night as well since I only just arrived. I'd meant to come for the entire party, but I was waylaid at my prior engagement."

"What was that?" She couldn't seem to stop from engaging with him. He was charming and so attractive, he made her teeth ache. Also, he was a man, and he was speaking to her and looking at her as no man ever had—not even Horatio. Creslow was regarding her as if he wanted to know all of her. In a short span of time, he'd somehow made her feel…special.

"I don't think I should tell you," he said with a devilish smirk. "It wouldn't be proper."

Did he think she was some green girl? Perhaps he really didn't know who she was, not that it mattered. "If it makes any difference to you, I am a widow."

"Are you?" His gaze dipped to her dressing gown. "Lavender. I should have realized. My apologies."

"Thank you, but that isn't necessary. Unless you had something to do with my husband's death?" she asked with a faint, wry smile. "He died of angina pectoris."

"I'm sorry for your loss. You can't have been married long."

Seven and a half years. "Long enough," she muttered. "I'm older than I look." When someone learned she was twenty-seven, they invariably stared at her in disbelief.

"Are you? I'm inclined to hazard a guess, but most ladies don't care to divulge their age. Instead, I shall answer your question. I was at a gentlemen's party. A friend is getting married next month, and we were celebrating his last days of bachelorhood."

"How did you manage to miscalculate your arrival at the house party?" Rebecca could well imagine. It had not been unusual for Horatio to forget to come home from his mistress's house.

One of Creslow's brows shot up. "Do I detect a note of sarcasm, as with your question about your husband's death?"

She kept herself from smiling. "Perhaps a small one."

"If you're perchance insinuating that our debauchery got the better of us, you may be right, but I swear it wasn't for the reasons you think. We were simply having too grand a time. We've been friends since those Eton days."

She liked his lack of guile. "These were your *Pamela* coconspirators?"

He laughed. "Just so."

"What reasons did you presume I was thinking?" Why was she practically flirting with this man? She hadn't done so in years, not since her first and only May Day Matchmaking Festival back in Marrywell.

And that hadn't turned out very well, despite an auspicious beginning. Charming and thoughtful, Horatio had danced attendance on Rebecca at the matchmaking festival. He was precisely what she was looking for: a kind and amiable gentleman with excellent prospects with which to support her and a family. Furthermore, marrying him would give her the chance to leave Marrywell and her unhappy childhood behind—the opportunity for a home and family of her own, a place where she would feel safe and, most of all, loved.

She might not have fallen deeply in love with him during the week of the festival, but they'd been smitten with each other, or so she'd thought. The promise of love had seemed bright and all but certain. Several months into the marriage, however, Horatio had revealed his true self—that of a lazy, self-indulgent hedonist.

"Let's see," the marquess mused, pondering her question. "I was at a gentlemen's celebration and missed most of my cousin's annual end-of-summer house party. I suspect you thought I'd been delayed by a woman."

"Or women," Rebecca murmured. This time, she couldn't keep a faint smirk from twisting her lips.

"Aha! You did think that!"

"For the reasons you stated, it seemed the most logical conclusion."

"My reputation precedes me, I take it." He sounded rather beleaguered.

"I am not aware of your reputation."

"Nearly rake status, I'm afraid. Not at all accurate, but it only takes one loose tongue to start a rumor." His gaze dipped to the book she held to her chest. "I'm keeping you from your reading."

Honestly, she was far more enthralled with him. "I still haven't decided if I'm taking the book," she said.

"Then may I interest you in a glass of sherry or whatever is on the cabinet over there?" He moved past her, nearly close enough for their arms to brush.

Nearly.

Rebecca set the book on a nearby table and followed him. Encountering him was by far the most interesting thing that had happened to her since Horatio's death. And this sort of interesting was definitely not *that* sort of interesting. The circumstances of her husband's death in the bed of his mistress had been rather horrifying. Because of that, no one had batted an eye when she'd appeared at a house party while still officially in half mourning. Indeed, she doubted anyone who knew the details of his demise would blame her if she resumed her normal life.

Too bad she didn't really have one. It was difficult when you were dependent on your husband's family because he'd left debt that, after settling, had rendered you penniless.

But Rebecca didn't want to think of any of that right now. She wanted to drink sherry—or whatever was available—with Lord Creslow.

Lord. Creslow.

He picked up each of the three decanters on the tray. "Looks like there is indeed sherry and also port. This last one..." He removed the top and sniffed, then promptly wrinkled his nose. "A very astringent madeira."

"Port, if you don't mind."

He poured two glasses of port and handed her

one. "To late-night—or is it early morning?—encounters."

Rebecca didn't pause to think how odd it was that she was toasting with a marquess in the middle of the night in a grand country house. She tapped her glass gently to his and sipped the rich, red, fortified wine.

He regarded her a moment. "You're a widow who survived an unhappy marriage, and I'm a rumored rake. And we've met in the middle of the night in a dim library. What do you suppose the gossip would be if we were found out?"

All sorts of lurid things came to mind. Rebecca drank more port, but swallowed too much and promptly coughed.

"Blast," he murmured, setting his glass down on the cabinet as he moved toward her. Taking her glass, he put his hand on her back and gave her a few pats. "That was my fault."

Rebecca gave him a puzzled look. "How can that be? I just sipped too great a quantity." She inhaled and was glad she didn't continue to cough.

He continued to stroke her back, and what had started as a comforting measure became something...more. Rebecca turned her head slightly, and their gazes locked. His hand stilled against her spine.

"I should go up to bed," she murmured, perhaps putting more emphasis on the word *should* than necessary.

"What about your book?" he asked.

"Given the lateness of the hour and the fact that we're leaving tomorrow, I ought to try to sleep."

"Try? Were you having trouble? Is that why you came down here?"

"Yes. I sometimes have difficulty sleeping, particularly in places other than my own bed." Why was she sharing so much with this stranger?

"That's a shame." His focus dropped to her mouth. "I imagine you've tried any number of remedies."

She had, in fact, but wouldn't bore him with the list. "Yes, though I'm always eager for a new suggestion. If you have one."

"I find sexual intercourse is the best way for me to fall right to sleep." His lips curled into a seductive smile. "The deep satisfaction just settles into my bones, and my body relaxes until I'm delivered into Morpheus's arms."

Had he just said *sexual intercourse*? She'd barely heard anything after that.

"Have I shocked you?" he whispered. Had he moved closer? "My apologies. I am rather swept up in this intimate moment we are sharing."

Rebecca swallowed, her heart thudding frantically. "I am too, but how does it end? I'm afraid I've no experience outside my marriage and that was woefully devoid of any such romance."

His brow puckered as he leaned even closer. "That is criminal. There are many ways this could end, and that is entirely up to you. I would suggest it *start* with a kiss. If you're amenable."

She feared she might expire if he didn't close the scant distance between them and kiss her. "I think it actually started the moment you touched my hand on the book."

His brow cocked up, and it seemed to lift the edge of his mouth along with it. "You may be right. I confess, when I saw you standing near the bookcase in your dressing gown, your stunning red curls escaping their plait, I felt immediately drawn to you. That you are as engaging as you are beautiful has made it impossible for me to leave, though I know I should. I am not typically *this* forward, whatever the gossips may say."

"I haven't heard a thing about you." Nothing beyond him being cousin to her hostess, anyway. She licked her lower lip, almost desperate to taste him. She'd never experienced a desire such as this.

His eyes slitted and his nostrils flared. "Now you've done it."

"What?"

"You've shown me your tongue, and now I simply *must* kiss you. Final chance to tell me to go away."

That was the last thing she wanted. "Kiss me."

"A woman who knows what she wants. How utterly captivating." His hand had remained against her back and now his palm pressed into her spine. His other arm snaked around her waist and pulled them flush together.

He smiled—with a hint of victory or anticipation or perhaps both—just before his mouth took hers. Rebecca clasped his waist with one hand and slid the other up to his warm neck. His lips molded to hers, guiding her in a kiss so sensual, she feared her knees might buckle.

This was entirely new territory. When Horatio had deigned to kiss her, he'd slobbered his mouth over hers and jabbed his tongue into her mouth. There'd been nothing arousing about it. But Creslow's kiss was an entirely different breed. He brought heat and desire. His lips opened against hers, and she stiffened.

"Something wrong?" he murmured as he kissed the corner of her mouth and then her jaw.

Rebecca cursed her reaction and was glad he hadn't pulled away, but then she was clutching him rather tightly. "I'm realizing my husband didn't know how to kiss."

"No romance and poor kissing skills. Please tell me he had a bounty of other redeeming qualities."

"I'm afraid not."

Creslow's features creased in a faint grimace. "I might wonder if you're relieved that he's gone."

"Relief barely scratches the surface. Perhaps you could continue so I may at least learn how to kiss properly?" *Please.*

"It would be my honor." His lips met hers once more, and this time when he opened and licked into her mouth, she pressed against him and wrapped her hand more firmly around his nape.

The kiss was decadent and lush, sweeping straight to the very core of her being. Her body quivered with newfound need. He held her with a raw possession, his hands caressing and seeking, that made her yearn for more.

Kiss after kiss sent her further into a mindless bliss. She was vaguely aware of him steering her backward and then in a new direction until she felt a piece of furniture at the back of her knees. He lowered her until she was perched on something. Slitting her eyes, she saw that it was a settee.

He turned her and guided her to lie back. "Is this all right?" he asked softly, his hands stroking her sides and hips.

"Yes," she whispered, breathless. "What are you going to do?"

"What would you like me to do?"

"I...I'm not sure. I enjoyed the kissing." She had to think she would also enjoy the sexual act itself, certainly more than she ever had with Horatio. She'd had to learn to find release on her own, for he'd never been able to provide pleasure, let alone satisfaction.

He leaned over her, planting his knee between hers on the settee. "You'll tell me if you want me to stop at any moment? I don't wish to overstep."

She couldn't imagine him doing that. Everything he'd done so far was wonderful. She clasped his head and pulled him down for another kiss. "Take the largest steps you like."

He teased and plundered her mouth until she was fairly drunk on his kisses. Not too far gone, however, that she wasn't aware of him unfastening her dressing gown. He pushed the garment open at her abdomen, and his hands came up to gently slide it over her breasts. His fingers grazed her, though the lawn of her night rail kept their skin from touching. Still, Rebecca's nipples tightened, and her entire body clenched with need.

Cupping her, he caressed one breast as his kisses trailed down her throat. With a gentle tug, he exposed the globe. His lips found their way to the swell, then he licked to her nipple. She tightened her grip on his head. He closed his mouth over her and suckled, making her arch up from the settee with a sharp intake of breath.

A swift and desperate arousal careened through her. Her hips moved, nearly of their own volition, as she sought gratification. His knee moved up, pressing against her sex, giving her pressure where she needed it most.

Rebecca reveled in his mouth on her breast and the stroke of his hand against her hip. He lifted the hem of her night rail, and the delightful press of his knee disappeared. She whimpered softly, but then his hand was between her thighs. He stroked her sex, almost cautiously at first, then with more demand. He focused his attention on the nub at the top—the place Horatio never seemed to realize existed—and drove her into a frenzy of desire.

His mouth left her breast, prompting her to whimper once more. Her nipple felt swollen and wonderfully heavy. The sensation carried through her, weighing her body with a hunger she'd never experienced.

She tangled her fingers in his thick hair as he moved down her body. He gently pushed her thighs wider apart just before his lips descended on her there. Did he mean to...? She was aware of this act, but Horatio had never done it. And honestly, the thought of him doing it had repulsed her. But this, Creslow's head buried between her thighs, was a forbidden desire she'd never expected.

His breath caressed her sex just before he licked her. Rebecca bit her lip to keep from crying out. She dug her fingers into his head as her hips twitched.

He moved his hand beneath her backside, lifting her for his feast as his lips and tongue delivered a devastating havoc on her sex. She couldn't keep from moving, from seeking that which was so close. But this was vastly different from anything she'd ever experienced. It wasn't a difficult climb to find the pinnacle. This was a torrent of sensation and pleasure, sending her racing toward completion.

As he suckled the nub, he slid his finger into her sex. She couldn't keep from crying out then. Her body shook with the storm, the impending crash. He brought her leg over his shoulder and gave her everything she needed.

Her world exploded with fire and ecstasy. He held her, his hand clasping her thigh as he guided her through the beautiful ravishment he'd visited upon her. Rebecca knew in that moment that her life was forever changed. She didn't have to settle or be grateful for what she'd been given. There was more out there in the world—happiness, self-indulgence, the absolutely unexpected.

When her body quieted, he moved away from her, pulling her night rail back over her sex. Rebecca's legs felt as though they were made of jelly. She looked up at him, seated at the other end of the settee, his body angled toward her. He wore a devilishly captivating, almost smug smile, and his banyan was slightly askew. Despite her extreme satisfaction, she was actually growing aroused again just looking at him.

"I suspect you'll sleep better tonight," he said. "At least, I hope so."

Given how languorous her limbs felt, she had to agree. "I feel as though you've given me a great gift. I've never had that before."

His brows drew together, and he leaned slightly forward. "Which part? I mean, that particular act or, and I hate to think this since you were married, the experience of an orgasm?"

Finally, she understood that word. "Both, really. I have found release, but only by my own hand."

Anger flashed across his features. "Your husband was clearly a selfish pig."

Now more than ever, Rebecca didn't want to think of Horatio. "I'm not selfish. How can I return this delightful gift you've given me?"

Before he could respond, a sound from the doorway made them both sit up straight. Rebecca drew her dressing gown tightly about herself.

A footman stood at the entrance to the library, his gaze trained on the hearth. "I beg your pardon," he said. "This is my last stop before turning in."

"It's quite all right," Creslow said casually as he rose from the settee. He offered his hand to Rebecca. The moment her palm touched his, she wanted to slide her hand farther up his arm and draw him close. She wanted to explore every part of him.

Would he invite her to his bed? It was a house party after all.

"Ah, Lord Creslow, that is you." The footman spoke hesitantly, almost nervously. "Your presence was requested in the billiards room. I just came from there, and a few gentlemen were hoping you'd return. Indeed, I think one was planning to rouse you from your slumber." He paused before adding, "I'll return in a few minutes." Then he hastily retreated.

The marquess muttered something. He turned to Rebecca, his thumb stroking her hand. Was he aware of the caress, or did he do it without thought? "I'm afraid I must go and see to whichever drunken fellow is seeking me out, not that I'm dressed for it." He glanced down at himself before meeting her gaze once more. "I thank you for a most spectacular encounter." He leaned toward her and brushed his lips against hers.

Rebecca took her free hand and clasped his shoulder, holding him while she deepened the kiss for a brief moment. When at last she pulled back, he regarded her with a heat that only stoked her arousal. She looked forward to seeing him tomorrow—and perhaps some time after that.

And for what? A torrid affair?

She'd be more than agreeable.

"You go first," he said, letting go of her hand. "We shouldn't be seen together—the footman's arrival was inopportune enough."

Rebecca wanted to say that her reputation wouldn't suffer, but she was a widow still in half mourning. While it might be acceptable for her to attend a local house party, it would be improper for her to be seen cavorting about in the middle of the night with a handsome marquess.

"Thank you," she said softly. "I shall sleep better than ever, I suspect. Good night." She forced herself to leave and instead focus on, hopefully, their next encounter.

"Good night," he called after her.

She turned at the doorway, and the image of him standing there, his dark hair tousled and the faint outline of his aroused cock creasing his garments, seared into her mind. Then she turned and left.

When she entered her room, she couldn't help but glance toward the wall separating her chamber from Aunt Jennet's. As much as Rebecca had detested Horatio, she adored his Aunt Jennet, who'd been nothing but kind, including bringing Rebecca to this house party, where she'd had a completely unexpected and amazing encounter.

Perhaps even life-changing.

She'd got a glimpse of what she'd missed being married to Horatio, and for the first time, she wondered if she might want to try that again. Marriage. Perhaps this time she could be certain there was love.

Her mourning period would end in January, and then she could decide what to do. In the meantime, she was grateful for Aunt Jennet's generosity, and she would do what she could to support a match between Delia and the young gentleman.

Beyond that, Rebecca would look forward to making a home for herself and perhaps even finding love. Did that include the love of her family back in Marrywell?

Once she'd escaped the coldness of her childhood home, she'd never expected to return. She'd also never expected her marriage to be as disappointing as it had been or that her husband would die, leaving her childless and without means.

She *could* go home…

Her ruthless mother was gone—sent away by Rebecca's younger sister with a tidy sum upon which to live. That sister, Leah, had returned to Marrywell and married the man she'd loved for practically forever. How wonderful it would to be to see her sister so happy, but painful too, since Rebecca wanted that and doubted she'd be so lucky. Which was fine. Leah deserved that joy more than anyone.

Rebecca's insides twisted. Whenever she thought of returning, she felt queasy. Facing Leah meant confronting a past of which Rebecca was terribly ashamed.

Better to look forward. If that future happened to include the deliriously wonderful Marquess of Creslow, Rebecca would have no complaints.

However, an affair with the marquess was not an occupation nor was it a marriage. And she couldn't keep living off Aunt Jennet's good will. If her sister Leah could make her way outside Marrywell as a paid companion—which was how she'd left several years ago before returning last spring—then Rebecca could find...something.

The question was, what would that something be?

CHAPTER 2

Seven months later

*R*ebecca set aside the letter from her older
sister, Meg, and pondered what she might
write in response. She was always purposely vague
when sharing the events of her life, which typically
weren't exciting. However, over the past six months
or so, many things had happened to shift Rebecca's
path from dull and unknown to unexpected and potentially exciting.

Unfortunately, none of it had a thing to do with
the Marquess of Creslow.

She had not seen him since their encounter in the
library at Clipstone Hedge. Aunt Jennet had wished
to leave fairly early the following day, which meant
they'd departed before the marquess had even come
downstairs.

There had been no good reason for Rebecca to
ask after him, so she hadn't. Nor had he come in
search of her. Rebecca had seen Lady Philpott so-
cially on several occasions since, including over the

holidays, but the marquess hadn't come up in conversation, save to say that he was in London.

The lack of a subsequent meeting had been disappointing, but really, Rebecca should not have expected it. Instead, she'd put her focus and energy into determining her future. As it happened, that future had begun at that same house party—just not with the marquess.

Rebecca's efforts to bring Delia and her now husband together had proven most successful. It had taken a month after the party to solidify the match, but Rebecca had enjoyed every moment of watching them fall in love. They'd wed in early November and were already expecting their first child.

After that success, Lady Philpott herself had *hired* Rebecca to find a match for her granddaughter. As a result of Rebecca's matchmaking, Ursula Philpott had married a wealthy gentleman who'd visited family in Leighton Buzzard over the holidays. Their wedding in February had sparked yet another match Rebecca had facilitated between another couple who'd attended the breakfast following the ceremony.

It seemed Rebecca had found her occupation. Being a matchmaker meant she could soon establish her own household. If she couldn't have a family, she could at least finally have a home.

Rebecca had saved the money she'd earned so far, and after another success or two, she'd be able to obtain lodgings either in Leighton Buzzard or perhaps the larger Luton. Aunt Jennet had been incredibly supportive and suggested Rebecca could go to London, but that didn't seem possible. At least for now.

As if conjured by Rebecca's thoughts, the woman swanned into the downstairs sitting room where Rebecca liked to complete her correspondence. "Ah, there you are, dear! I've just received the best news."

She waved a piece of parchment in the air before moving to perch on a chair near the writing desk.

In her late fifties, with nearly gray hair, Jennet St. James was as joyful as her nephew had been dull. Her walnut-brown eyes nearly always sparkled with at least a hint of merriment in her pale countenance, and she strove to make everyone around her smile. It wasn't difficult when one was blessed with such an amiable disposition. She'd been the one bright spot for Rebecca since she'd left Marrywell to wed Horatio.

"What news is that?" Rebecca asked with a smile.

Aunt Jennet folded the parchment and set it on her lap. "You've had an inquiry regarding your matchmaking services. Susan—Lady Philpott—has just informed me that her cousin, Lord Creslow, would like to engage your services."

The breath left Rebecca's lungs. Of all the people in England...

Lord Creslow. *Him.*

She wanted to know about the marquess, but first asked, "Why did Lady Philpott ask you instead of me?"

"She wanted to make sure you were available. I may have led her to believe that your matchmaking expertise is in demand. Because it *is*." Aunt Jennet gave her a confident smile. "Or it will be as soon as you decide to advertise your services."

"I do appreciate you speaking so kindly of me," Rebecca said. "You have already been so generous."

"You like matchmaking, don't you? I hope you don't think you need to find something to do in order to leave here—you are welcome here as long as you like. Forever, even."

"I *do* like matchmaking. Very much." Rebecca found it wonderfully satisfying. "I appreciate all you've done for me, and while I have been happy here, it's time for me to see what else life has in store."

"I admire your sense of adventure. It is unsurprising. It's not every young woman who accepts an offer of marriage and agrees to move far away from home without even knowing if she'll like where she's going." Aunt Jennet's face creased with understanding. "I know things didn't happen as you'd hoped, and for that, I am deeply sorry. I do hope you've been able to heal and recover."

Rebecca knew she wasn't referring to Horatio's death, but to his treatment of her during their marriage. Aunt Jennet had been aware of Horatio's philandering, and Rebecca had disclosed some of his other awfulness. Horrified, Aunt Jennet apologized for him over and over, despite Rebecca insisting she needn't do so.

Now, Rebecca wanted to ask about the marquess. "I didn't realize his lordship was in the market for a wife." She posed the question calmly, but inside, she was a riot of anticipation and excitement at the prospect of seeing him again.

Except it would be to find him a wife. That settled on her like a cold, wet blanket.

"He's decided it's time to remarry, get on with his duty and all that," Aunt Jennet replied.

*Re*marry? How had Rebecca not known that he was a widower? "I didn't know he'd been married before."

"She died about eighteen months into the marriage, I believe. He retreated for a year of mourning, and when he returned to Society, he seemed fine, though Susan says he's never quite regained his former exuberance, that if you look hard enough, there's a slight shadow that clings to him."

Rebecca hadn't seen that, but she'd spent hardly any time with him. And the time they had spent together had been splendid, if not exuberant. "I'm sorry to hear his marriage ended in that way." Had he loved his wife, then? Rebecca hoped so, but then she imagined the loss would have been devastating.

"I'd be honored to help him find a new marchioness," Rebecca said.

"I was hoping you'd say that." Aunt Jennet let her smile fade and adopted a businesslike tone. "Creslow doesn't wish to find a match in London. He says there is no one of interest to him there this Season. He considered coming back here, which is why Susan thought you could be of assistance after making successful matches in the area."

Rebecca wasn't sure she could think of anyone in or around Leighton Buzzard that would be a good match for the marquess. It was too bad they didn't have a May Day Matchmaking Festival like Marrywell where she grew up. The festival started in less than a month…

Could she even think of returning home? The thought made her feel both unsettled and excited. Mostly unsettled. But there was perhaps no better time or reason. She could use the festival and her position as a matchmaker as an excuse to return, and if things were unpleasant, well, the festival only lasted a week.

"You look as though you already have someone in mind," Aunt Jennet said.

"Not someone. Some*where*. I wonder if the marquess would be interested in attending the Marrywell May Day Matchmaking Festival. There will be scores of ladies looking to fall in love and marry. There is no better place or time to find a mate." Rebecca's throat dried up. She'd believed in that her whole life —that Marrywell's matchmaking festival was magic and that it would deliver her from her miserable family.

And it had, only right into a miserable marriage.

Rebecca reminded herself that she was not the norm, that the vast majority of people at the festival made loving matches. Just because it hadn't been the case for her, didn't mean she couldn't ensure that it was for the marquess. She'd already proven that she could match others better than she could herself.

Summoning her courage before she could change her mind, she gave Aunt Jennet a level stare. "Do you think he would be interested in attending the Marrywell Matchmaking Festival?"

Aunt Jennet clapped her hands together. "What a marvelous idea. I didn't even think of that. I'll have Susan ask him."

Matchmaking a marquess would be just the thing to launch Rebecca in this career. The future she wanted—her own home, no one she had to rely on, and no one who would let her down—would be within her grasp.

Suddenly, Aunt Jennet reached over and touched Rebecca's hand. "Please forgive me, I'm managing this when I should not. You write to Susan and tell her what you're thinking. Or we can go visit her."

Rebecca gave her a warm smile and put her hand over Aunt Jennet's. "I do not feel managed. I appreciate your kindness and your help. I'll write to Susan directly, since we'll need to organize things quickly if we're to get to Marrywell before the first when the festival begins. I'll include that I'm available to meet with her if she'd like."

"Excellent." Aunt Jennet sniffed and looked at her with pride. "You're going to be marvelous, and soon your matchmaking services will be in such high demand that you'll need to hire a secretary simply to deal with the inquiries."

Rebecca laughed. "I should like that."

An uneasy anticipation settled within her. It was

because she might be returning home. Or because she would be finding a bride for the man with whom she'd hoped to have a liaison.

She needed to put him out of her mind—at least in that way. Thinking of their evening together in the library would not be appropriate as she sought to match him.

They would forge a professional relationship, far different from the way they'd started. While it would be difficult for Rebecca, she would do it. She had to.

And what of him? Had he thought of her at all? What would he say when his cousin suggested he hire the woman he'd pleasured in the library as his matchmaker? Not that Lady Philpott was aware of that, of course.

It was entirely possible Creslow wouldn't connect the two at all. He hadn't even known Rebecca's name that night.

Since time was short, they could very well meet in Marrywell as strangers. Well, not as strangers. Because as soon as he saw her, he'd realize who she was. And what if he didn't want her to be his matchmaker? Then she would have traveled all that way for nothing.

Not for *nothing*, since she could always call on her family… This scheme suddenly seemed ill-conceived. Yet, she couldn't deny she wanted to do it. To return to Marrywell and visit her family. To see the marquess again and help him find happiness.

To determine if there was, perchance, any happiness for her.

~

Late April, Marrywell

*B*enjamin Nash, the Marquess of Creslow, stepped out of his coach into the sun-dappled late afternoon on a quiet side street in the quaint town of Marrywell in Hampshire. A day's ride from London, it was close enough to feel like a short jaunt and yet distant enough to seem rural and removed.

Although, given the number of inns and public houses and the quantity of people bustling about, the place appeared somewhat like a resort town. Because visitors, including Nash, were flooding into the popular matchmaking festival.

He'd barely managed to secure a room at what was purportedly the newest lodging. It was also rather small when compared with those that stood along the High Street. The Buck and Maiden was perhaps a trifle too cleverly named, but it was a charming structure with three storeys, the uppermost of which sported three dormered windows. He hoped his hastily arranged room wasn't crammed beneath the roof.

His matchmaker, hired at the behest of his cousin Susan, Lady Philpott, was also staying here. Nash had scoffed at the idea of a matchmaker at first, but it hadn't taken him long to realize she would be a great help given the sort of marriage he was looking for. Susan had assured him that Mrs. Rebecca Sweet was excellent at finding just the right match.

Nash doubted Sweet was her real name. It was too perfect for a matchmaker. He tipped his hat to her for taking such a pleasing moniker. Would she look as amenable as her surname, however? He envisioned a middle-aged woman with spectacles and a dignified demeanor. Well, he'd find out shortly.

A groom came from the stable yard to help Nash's coachman, and Nash made his way to the door of the inn. He hadn't brought his valet, a decision he might yet regret. However, the young man's mother was ill, and Nash could see the lad was worried to leave London. So, Nash had insisted he stay and care for her. As it happened, when Nash's secretary had reserved the room, the innkeeper had written that personal assistance would be available if necessary. Nash hoped that meant someone might draw him a bath or help with his clothing.

The door opened just as Nash arrived at the threshold. "Welcome, my lord." The innkeeper, Mr. Thomason, a stout gentleman in his forties garbed in an immaculate costume of dark blue, possessed a sharp, assessing gaze. The man greeted Nash with a nod. "We are pleased you have chosen to stay at the Buck and Maiden."

Nash didn't point out that there hadn't been any other choice. "I understand this is a new establishment. I am delighted to be among your first guests."

Mr. Thomason smiled. "This is our inaugural festival. We may be smaller than some of the other lodgings in Marrywell, but I think you will find that our amenities are exemplary. Allow me to show you to your chamber, where you have your own dressing and bathing room."

"Indeed? How splendid."

"Will you require valet service?" Mr. Thomason asked.

"On occasion. Thank you." Nash followed him to the wide, polished staircase.

They climbed to the first floor, and the innkeeper led him to the right. They followed the corridor to the last door, also on the right. Opening the door, Mr. Thomason gestured for Nash to precede him.

"This is our finest suite, my lord," Mr. Thomason said as Nash took in the chamber.

They'd stepped into a small sitting room decorated in blue and gold. The furniture was bright and new, the carpet vividly colored with blues, golds, and rich browns.

Mr. Thomason indicated an open doorway to the left. "Through there is the bedchamber as well as the dressing and bathing room. There is an access door for the footman to fill the bath at your request. Our valet will also come through that way. You are free to lock it for privacy at any time, of course."

"You've seen to every need. I'm most impressed." Nash turned about, surveying the room. There was another door on the right side. "Where does that lead?"

"As this is our largest and best suite, there is a second bedroom. However, since you didn't require it, we've placed another guest there. The door is locked from both sides, so you shan't bother each other."

"Very efficient."

"The footman will place your cases in the dressing room. Would you like the valet to unpack your things?"

"I would, thank you." Nash could scarcely believe he was in rural Hampshire.

"As you like," Mr. Thomason said. "Can I offer you any refreshment?"

"That would not come amiss. I wonder, has Mrs. Sweet arrived? I am to meet with her before dinner."

"Indeed, she has, my lord. In fact, she is in the room next door." The innkeeper glanced toward the closed door leading to the other bedroom. "I did not realize you were associated with one another."

"How convenient—she is my matchmaker." Except Nash didn't particularly want to invite her into his personal quarters. That seemed indecorous. "Would you mind informing her that I am here? I will take refreshment in the common room, and she can join me there."

"Certainly. I'll do that straightaway." Mr. Thomason left, closing the door behind him.

Nash removed his hat and gloves and walked into the bedchamber. The four-poster bed gleamed with polish and was elegantly dressed in dark blue and gold. There was a low fire burning in the grate, lending a cozy air to the room. He moved to the window, which overlooked the small garden to the rear of the inn. Flowers bloomed in formal beds, and a few benches were placed strategically about. Mr. Thomason had obviously worked hard and spared no expense to create a most pleasing establishment.

Making his way into the dressing room, Nash was impressed again by the amenities. The tub looked most inviting. Or it would when there was steaming water in it later. He set his hat and gloves on the dresser and turned to go downstairs.

Time to meet the matchmaker.

Perhaps he'd even encounter her in the corridor on his way down. But he did not.

He was first to arrive in the empty common room and chose a table set in front of a window looking out at the back garden. He sat so that he faced the staircase.

"Good afternoon, my lord." A woman in her forties arrived at Nash's table and set down a tray with tea, sandwiches, and cakes. She smiled warmly. "Welcome to Marrywell. I'm Mrs. Thomason. If you're here to find a love match, I offer my heartfelt hope for your success."

A *love* match. No, that wasn't what he wanted. He needed a marchioness. Love would not play any part of the transaction. He'd done that before, and his heart simply couldn't endure another loss. The despair he'd suffered both during his wife's illness and after her death barely eighteen months into their marriage had broken him. If he was even capable of loving again, he didn't want to. The risk was simply too great, the pain of loss too devastating.

After tucking himself away at Creslow Manor for a year, he'd surrendered to his mother's persuasion to rejoin Society. He'd pasted a smile atop his grief and pretended that all was well. Four years on, he was still hiding behind a façade and suspected he always would. It was much more comfortable in this space where no one got too close, and he didn't recall the past.

"I am here to find a bride, yes," Nash confirmed since Mr. Thomason would no doubt inform his wife that Mrs. Sweet was Nash's matchmaker. His purpose in coming to Marrywell would then be obvious.

"You will be quite popular. I daresay you won't have a moment's peace," Mrs. Thomason said with a touch more glee than Nash would have liked. He was used to being popular in London, but he wasn't completely overrun. It sounded as if this matchmaking festival had the potential to be the Marriage Mart if it were overfed and overgrown into the size of a giant. "Have you given any thought to the sort of bride you're seeking?"

An image of the alluring widow Nash had encountered at Clipstone Hedge all those months ago rose in his mind. She'd haunted his dreams on many occasions. Their time together had been cut short, and he felt as though things between them were unfinished. Unfortunately, they would remain that way since he didn't even know who she was.

Before Nash could think of how to respond, Mrs. Thomason's gaze moved to the staircase. "Ah, here is Mrs. Sweet. Please excuse me." She swept away, and Nash rose to greet his matchmaker.

The moment his gaze met hers, he nearly choked on his own inhalation.

This was Mrs. Sweet?

This was the woman who'd invaded his dreams, who'd made it impossible for him to find more than the most basic satisfaction with another woman. Not completing their night together was one of the greatest regrets of his life.

"You." That was the only word he could manage, apparently.

She, on the other hand, did not look surprised to see him. A serene smile lifted her pink lips. "Good afternoon, Lord Creslow. It's a pleasure to see you again."

Her blue eyes looked over him, but didn't linger, as if she quickly assessed what she saw and found it merely adequate. Instead of the plait she'd sported that night in the library, her red hair was coiled into a prim style. She wore a smooth expression, her ivory complexion accented with a few freckles on the bridge of her nose. Dressed in a smart but simple gray frock trimmed in green, she appeared appropriately businesslike. And yet, he kept picturing her in that lavender dressing gown. Now he was recalling how he'd pushed the garment apart so he could more easily access her lush body. *Hell.* He was growing hard. This would not do.

"You must forgive me, Mrs. Sweet. I was not expecting *you*."

She arched a red brow. "I wondered if that may be the case. I had the distinct impression at our last meeting that you were not aware of my identity."

No, he hadn't been, and now he felt like a crass idiot. "My apologies. My only excuse is that I was rather swept away. You, however, knew precisely who I was."

"I did." Directing her focus away from him, she surveyed the table. "It's best if we don't discuss that event. It's hardly germane to our business." She met his gaze. "I do apologize for not writing to inform you of my identity. As you are aware, we were pressed for time with arranging to get here for the festival."

She put her hand on the chair opposite the one he'd vacated, and he rushed to hold it for her as she sat down. His fingertips were very close to her head. They fairly itched to touch her.

No, this would not do *at all*.

Nash took his seat opposite her. "No need to apologize."

"But what if you would have preferred not to hire me?" Small but bright spots of pink bloomed in her cheeks. "I will understand if you wish to change your mind."

"Why on earth would I do that? My cousin says you are an excellent matchmaker."

"That is most kind of her. It's just... I may not have given you the best impression when we first met."

He told himself not to flirt with her. "Your impression was no worse than mine. In any case, I have nothing but the best impression from our first encounter." He suppressed a smile, for then she would think he *was* flirting. How he wanted to. But he would settle for telling her the truth, which he had.

"We can start anew, then?" she asked.

The urge to pick up where they'd left off was nearly overwhelming, but Nash could not do that with his matchmaker. No matter how badly he wanted to. "Yes. I am most pleased to make your acquaintance and to have you as my matchmaker."

She smiled brightly. "Thank you. I am delighted to be of assistance. Shall I pour?" Her voice was not at all how he remembered. She sounded like a proper miss, er, madam, instead of a velvet-toned siren. Or perhaps that was just how he'd cast her in his head. And now he needed to cast that *out* of his head.

"Yes, please."

She poured out their cups and added milk and a scant amount of sugar.

He took his cup from the tray and set it in front of him. "You know how I like my tea," he murmured.

"Purely coincidence. I know very little about you, and nothing that would pertain to finding you a match, which is why I requested we meet before the festival begins. I need to understand what you're looking for in a wife so that I may find the right match." She gave him a pert look as she picked up her tea for a small sip.

Nash averted his gaze from her mouth. He could still taste her plump, kissable lips. How was he going to get past this distraction?

She, on the contrary, didn't seem troubled at all. Perhaps she didn't hold that encounter in the same reverence as he did. All the more reason for him to put it behind him and focus on the matter at hand.

Finding a marchioness.

He sipped his tea and took a small plate from the tray, upon which he immediately placed a sandwich. "What would you like to know?"

Mrs. Sweet pulled a small notebook and a pencil from her pocket. "Since I don't have…much experience with you, I should like to spend tonight and tomorrow getting to know you as well as I can. This will help me recognize what sort of wife would complement you."

He sensed her hesitation regarding their…experience. Perhaps she wasn't as immune to that night as he'd thought. Or mayhap she simply felt awkward about it. Hell, it *was* awkward.

Even so, he wanted to jest about spending tonight together, but he decided that would only make things even more uncomfortable. "That is acceptable." How formal he sounded. But what else could he be?

"What can you tell me about the woman who will most please you? I understand you were married before. Perhaps you could tell me about her and—"

"No." He picked up his utensils and cut a bite of sandwich since he had no intention to say more. He couldn't bear another woman like Louisa, a wife he could love so deeply that she would completely devastate what was left of him if she too died.

Her brows drew together. "It would be helpful." She took a plate and a sandwich for herself.

"I prefer to look forward, not back," he said after swallowing. "I would like a wife who isn't too young —no one who's just left the schoolroom. I admire a woman with intelligence, curiosity, and a sense of humor." Levity had been his most cherished friend since Louisa had died.

Mrs. Sweet scratched out a few notes in her book. She did not look up as she asked, "What are your interests?"

"Reading." Too late, he realized she might think he was saying that to recall what had brought them together in the library.

She glanced up, but her expression was unreadable. "Novels? Crop treatises? Newspapers?"

"All of those. I also like poetry."

She continued to write without looking at him. "Do you prefer a lady who lives in London or who was reared in a particular way?"

"London is not a requirement, and I've no demands about a woman's background."

Mrs. Sweet set her pencil down and regarded him across the table. "You're shopping for a marchioness. You have no requirements as to her upbringing?"

He made a face. "Shopping is such a cold word." Except it was entirely accurate, especially in his case. Procuring might even be better. He took another bite of the ham sandwich.

She said nothing, but cut and took a bite of her sandwich. Apparently, she was waiting for him to respond to her query. He swallowed and leaned back slightly against the chair. "I don't need to marry a duke's daughter, if that's what you're getting at. She ought to be comfortable in a London drawing room or attending a ball with notable figures."

"What does that mean?" She dabbed the napkin to her mouth, and he had to tear his gaze away from her lips again.

"I sit in the Lords. I know a great many…important people. Occasionally, we will need to socialize with them."

"Certainly." Setting down her fork, she plucked up her pencil once more and made additional notes in her book. "I'm sure you'll think of other things to add, and as I get to know you, I'll hopefully develop a sense of what sort of female will appeal to your sensibilities."

You appeal to me.

The thought leapt straight to his tongue, but he managed to keep it to himself. Barely.

She set her pencil down. "Allow me to explain how the festival works. It lasts a week, which I'm sure you know. On the first day, there is a welcome reception at the assembly hall where all ladies seeking to wed will appear. This is so the May Queen can choose her court of seven maidens fair. Those ladies will be the most sought-after of the festival."

A court? Maidens fair? "Why?"

She blinked at him. "Because they just are."

He leaned forward. "How does the queen choose them? Is it based on their station? Beauty? Wealth? Charm? Dare I hope, wittiness?"

"It is up to each individual queen how she selects her court."

"Well, that's bloody arbitrary. What if the queen

simply chooses her family members or close friends?"

"That has, ah, happened on occasion."

He leaned forward. "Or what if someone bribes the queen to choose them?"

Her eyes flickered with surprise. "I've never heard of that happening."

"I'd wager it has." He snorted. "If it's just the same to you, I see no advantage to putting any importance on these maidens who are chosen for some unknown reason."

"I should caution you that the people of Marrywell take the festival and its traditions quite seriously. You may wish to refrain from sharing your opinion on the potential absurdity of the queen's court."

"I didn't say it was absurd."

She cocked her brow again. "But you were thinking that, weren't you?"

He couldn't help but smile. "You're getting to know me already."

She sipped her tea before continuing. "The queen's court is announced at the opening ball on the first day of the festival. The crowning ceremony will occur in the botanical gardens—there's a dais—if the weather is fair. If not, it will be held in the assembly rooms."

"This festival is serious business."

"Quite. Each day, there are a variety of activities to choose from, many of which take place in the botanical gardens. The most popular is the Grand Picnic. There are boats to be rowed on the small lake, and, of course, picnic blankets and food."

"No drink?" he asked wryly.

"The brewer's field is open all week."

He leaned forward once more. "The what now?" While he found the court and ceremonial crowning nonsensical, he could absolutely endorse a brewer's field.

"Brewers from the district come to share their ales. It can get rather boisterous there."

Nash couldn't help but be impressed with her knowledge, but then his cousin had told him that the matchmaker was from this town. "I understand you were born here. Do you attend the festival every year?"

She cut another small piece of sandwich. "Not since I met my former husband. That was nine years ago."

"But you've been to visit?" he asked while she was chewing. "You're familiar with some potential brides?"

It was a moment before she responded, "No. However, despite my lengthy absence, I will do my best to find someone appropriate. You must understand that there are no guarantees. Just because a lady seems like a good match doesn't mean you'll share that certain...spark that people look for. I'm afraid I can't conjure the perfect match."

"Nor do I expect you to," he said, appreciating her frankness. He owed it to her to be equally honest. "A spark will not be necessary. This is why I decided to hire a matchmaker. The most important requirement for my marriage is that there will be no emotional attachment. I would like to share a physical attraction, but that alone will be sufficient."

She stared at him a long moment. Then her lashes fluttered as she continued to regard him. "I want to make sure I understand. You don't want to fall in love?"

"Absolutely not." While it was necessary that he tell her this, he prayed she wouldn't pry for a reason. "I desire a marchioness who will enjoy the physical aspects of marriage and, hopefully, provide an heir.

She will need to understand that this is a business arrangement—one that is mutually beneficial. She will live a life of luxury and privilege. I can't think it will be difficult to find a woman who would want that."

"Perhaps not. However, the Marrywell festival has a long and legendary history of making love matches. It may be more challenging than you realize to find a lady interested in just a 'business arrangement.'" Her mouth tipped into a slight frown. "If I'd known this, I might have steered you elsewhere."

Did that mean she didn't want to help him? "Do you wish to resign your employment?"

Surprise flashed in her eyes. "No, not that." She shook her head. "I need to readjust my thinking. This is a matchmaking festival, but not *all* the matches are based on love. I'm confident we can find what you are looking for."

"Excellent. I have to think your connection to Marrywell will be of benefit. Will you be visiting your family? If they are still here?" He hoped he hadn't dredged up anything awful. What if they were dead? Christ, his mind could turn to the maudlin so easily if he wasn't careful.

"They are still here," she said slowly. "However, I have not maintained a close relationship with them. I'm sure I'll see them at some point."

She finished her sandwich, and Nash helped himself to a cake. When they were both done, she pushed back from the table. "I should like to retire before dinner."

"We'll dine together here?" he asked. At her nod, he added, "So we can get to know each other."

He had a hundred questions for her and not one of them had a thing to do with finding his future bride. Why wasn't she close to her family? Was there a reason she'd left Marrywell? What about her husband—the fool who'd squandered such a passionate wife? Nash had not forgotten that the man hadn't bothered to pleasure her.

Hell. Now he was thinking of *that* again, and his cock twitched.

"That will be fine," she said with an equanimity he didn't feel at the moment. Her presence was most upsetting. But in the most wondrous way.

He moved to hold her chair while she stood. "I'll escort you upstairs."

"That won't be necessary."

"Perhaps not, but since my room adjoins yours, I'll just be following you."

Her eyes rounded, and it was the most reaction he'd seen from her that day. "It *adjoins* mine?"

"Apparently, it is a two-bedroom suite, but since I am traveling alone, the innkeeper lodged you in the other bedroom. There's just a locked door between us." How dangerous and utterly provocative that sounded.

"I see. That is…convenient."

Nash grinned. "Precisely what I said." Though the meaning of that convenience had changed now that he knew who his matchmaker was.

How could he have not known? He felt like a fool. Would he still have hired her? Or would he have asked her to engage in an illicit and delightful affair?

He would never know, and perhaps that was for the best.

hough Rebecca had planned to rest before dinner, she'd been far too fraught after her meeting with Creslow. Instead, she kept finding herself staring at the door separating their rooms just as she was doing now.

Huffing out a breath, she turned and went to the small dressing room that adjoined her chamber. In there, she could be as far away from the marquess as possible. That felt much safer.

Because he seemed to still be thinking of their encounter last September. He'd definitely remembered her. She had to admit the look on his face when he'd seen her had been satisfying. There'd been shock, then recognition, then some sort of delight or enthusiasm, as if he were glad to finally lay eyes on her again. Perhaps he'd been wondering who she was, since he clearly hadn't known her name. Why, then, hadn't he asked his cousin?

The logical answer was that he hadn't really been thinking of her, that he'd forgotten about her entirely until that afternoon. Rebecca pressed her hand to her forehead. She was the one who needed to forget about that night.

She looked into the mirror at the dressing table.

Her round eyes stared back from her pale countenance. Her hair was barely contained in its style. Rebecca had pulled several curls free around her temples and ears because it was easier to just let them have their way now than allow them to escape the pins and pomade she'd used. Restraint was a word Rebecca knew well.

And she would be completely restrained when it came to the marquess. There would be no repeat of what they'd done before—upon their first meeting!

She'd expected to feel somewhat embarrassed upon seeing him again. Instead, an overwhelming heat and desire had stolen over her. The fact that he didn't appear troubled by their immediate and single liaison had likely helped matters. That and the sense that he'd wanted to perhaps flirt with her, but then seemed to decide against it.

In the end, Rebecca wasn't at all sure what the man was thinking. Perhaps that was for the best.

If he encouraged her in the slightest...well, she wasn't sure she'd be able to refuse him. Even though she *must*. This position was an excellent opportunity for her. If she successfully matched a marquess, she would likely have more clients than she could manage.

But that was only if she was successful, and after her initial meeting with the marquess, she had some doubts. He wanted the sort of marriage she'd had—a mutually beneficial arrangement with no emotional attachment but physical gratification. The latter had been absent from her marriage, but that was what Horatio had wanted: exactly what Creslow described. Did she want to be a part of fostering a union like that?

Not if it turned out as hers had done.

Granted, Horatio had wed Rebecca without stating his intentions. Creslow would have to be clear with potential brides. If not, Rebecca couldn't help him.

A knock sounded from the door—the one to her room from the corridor, *not* the one she shared with the marquess. Rebecca glanced at the gloves she'd laid out but ultimately decided not to bother with since they were only going downstairs to eat.

Spinning away from the dressing table, she hurried into the bedchamber. She paused and took a deep breath before opening the door. He stood in the corridor dressed in his impeccable evening finery, his mouth curved into a heart-stopping smile. Rebecca had to bite the inside of her cheek to keep from reacting. Then he raked his gaze over her, and she was glad he couldn't see the gooseflesh that rose on the back of her neck and her upper arms.

"You look lovely, Mrs. Sweet. I see you are no longer in half mourning. I wasn't entirely sure since your traveling costume was gray."

She'd altered a few of her mourning gowns, adding trim so that they would look less like mourning gowns. Actually, that had been Aunt Jennet's idea since Rebecca had balked at her spending yet more money on clothing for her degenerate nephew's widow. But Aunt Jennet always insisted on taking care of Rebecca, whether that was furnishing her with a mourning wardrobe, providing a roof over her head, or helping her find a new path in life.

"My year of mourning was finished in January." Rebecca stepped into the corridor and closed the door behind her.

"I'm pleased to hear it." He offered her his arm.

Rebecca hesitated. What would it be like to touch him again? It was probably better if she didn't. Instead, she said, "There's no need for us to be that formal. We are business associates." Shoulders back, she walked toward the staircase.

He joined alongside her. "I suppose that's true. I was only being gentlemanly, as I was raised to be."

Of course he was. He'd mentioned Eton at their last meeting. He'd likely gone on to Oxford or perhaps Cambridge. A nobleman would be finely educated in all matters.

Rebecca suddenly felt as though she were in the wrong place with the wrong person. What business did she have playing matchmaker to a *marquess*? She was a farmer's daughter with no notion of how the peerage lived, apart from the one house party she'd attended at the home of a baron. The word *impostor* flashed through her mind.

The common room, like the inn, wasn't large. There were six tables set about and a seating area near the wide hearth. A sitting room adjoined the chamber, via a door on the same wall as the staircase.

Unlike that afternoon, the common room contained other people besides them. Three of the tables were occupied—one by a pair of gentlemen, another by a mother and marriage-aged daughter, and the last by a family of four, which included the parents, another marriage-aged daughter, and a younger son, perhaps nine or ten, who tugged at his cravat.

Mrs. Thomason greeted them and showed them to a square table set for two. "Would you care for wine or ale?"

Creslow held Rebecca's chair while she sat, then moved to sit opposite her. He regarded her with an arched brow—how she remembered those wonderful, expressive eyebrows of his—and asked, "Port?"

She tried not to smile, really she did, but it was impossible. Her lips lifted. "I think I'll have sack instead. If that's available."

"Of course," Mrs. Thomason said. "And your lordship?"

"I'll be brazen and have the port."

The innkeeper's wife gave him a slightly bewildered look before taking herself off.

Rebecca looked over at him. She was torn between wishing he hadn't mentioned anything to do with their past evening together and enjoying the thrill of their shared memory. "She is going to wonder why you find port a bold choice."

"Perhaps I'm a dullard who rarely drinks."

"You certainly are not a dullard."

His lips spread in a wicked grin. "I'm pleased to hear you say so. Though, perhaps you'll alter your opinion after we get to know each other."

She would wager her future earnings that she would *not* change her mind. "I'm afraid if I come to that conclusion, I'll have to resign my position. I can't possibly dupe a lady into marrying a dullard."

He arched a brow at her. "You possess a charming morality, Mrs. Sweet."

Was he surprised by that because of how she'd behaved with him when they'd met? If so, it didn't seem to bother him since he'd plainly said he had no reservations about hiring her.

Mrs. Thomason returned with their wine and informed them that the dinner courses would start momentarily. Rebecca didn't want to continue that line of conversation with him.

So, she focused on what was important: doing what he'd hired her to do. "It looks to me that there are two marriageable women here in the common room. Perhaps you'll find whom you seek before the festival even begins."

He glanced toward the table where the family was sitting. "That one looks as if she just left her governess." He shook his head.

"You don't know if that's true. She may just *look* young. People often say that about me. Or, if she is young, she may be wise beyond her years. You can't discount someone out of hand based on your assumptions."

He exhaled. "I would agree with you, however I did say I want to have a physical attraction with my future bride, and I feel none toward that particular young lady. I mean no offense. You're either drawn to someone or you're not."

Rebecca hadn't realized how true that was until she'd met him. She'd never been drawn to anyone the way she'd been to him. It was as if he were the largest flower in the garden with the most nectar, and she was the most devoted bee.

She needed to stop thinking about how he made her feel and focus on what she'd been hired to do. He wanted a business arrangement with the benefits of a sexual relationship and, presumably, an heir.

"You do want a spark," she said. "Just one that is only physical in nature."

"I suppose that's true." His gaze lingered on her, and she wondered if he was thinking what she was: that they had shared a spark. "I would like our union to be mutually satisfying."

It was difficult not to think of her own marriage. That was what Horatio had wanted—a wife who would pleasure him, though her satisfaction didn't signify. And sons.

He'd determined relatively quickly that Rebecca didn't please him in bed, but he'd continued coming to her in the hope of getting her with child. After two years and no pregnancy, he'd left her alone. It was then that she'd confirmed her suspicions, that he kept a mistress. And he did so—though not the same woman—for the duration of their marriage. None of them had given him a child either, as far as Rebecca knew.

Would Creslow want a similar situation? He could have his proper marchioness who would bear his children, and he could keep a mistress. Rebecca couldn't support that. "Since you are primarily interested in a business arrangement, do you plan to take a mistress after your wife provides you with an heir?"

He'd picked up his wineglass, but paused with it halfway to his mouth. His jaw dropped as he stared at her. "I would *never.*"

She felt her cheeks warm and wished she could take the words back even as his words delighted her. "My apologies, my lord. I didn't mean to offend."

He took a long drink of port, then looked at the glass before moving his focus to Rebecca. "You did not offend me," he said at last after setting his glass down. "I can't find fault with your reasoning. A great many men of my station, and of others, I'm sure, do take mistresses. I'm just not that sort of man. My forthcoming marriage may be based on a mutually beneficial agreement instead of emotion, but I will still be loyal to my wife. Just as I expect she will remain loyal to me."

"You feel strongly about that," she said, hearing the conviction in his tone.

"Yes. My father was not a good example when it came to such things. Or, perhaps he was, because I vowed I would never do to my wife what he did to my mother."

Rebecca felt the emotional equivalent of swooning. "That's wonderful." His future wife would be very lucky, even without love between them.

Without love? Creslow might not want that, but Rebecca suspected it wouldn't be difficult for his wife to fall in love with him. What would he do if she simply couldn't help herself? And could he actually keep himself from succumbing to the emotion?

The uneasiness she'd felt earlier returned. "We will need to be explicit with potential brides. This is of the utmost importance. A woman should know what she's entering into."

His gaze softened. "You speak from experience."

"I do," she said simply, not wishing to elaborate and hoping he wouldn't ask her to.

"I agree. We must be precise in our communication in this endeavor. I trust you'll find just the right woman."

"I will try, my lord."

"You needn't call me 'my lord,'" he said. "I should like for you to call me Creslow. Or, if you prefer, you may call me Nash, which is how most of my friends address me."

Nash seemed far too intimate. But hadn't they already been that?

Mrs. Thomason brought white soup, and Rebecca focused on eating that for a moment while she tried to redirect her thoughts. She needed to search for a woman that he would find attractive. Which meant she should ask what attributes aroused him.

What if he described her?

He won't. He is your client. Stop thinking of him as your lover!

"Is there something wrong, Mrs. Sweet?" he asked, his brow furrowed.

"No. I'm merely thinking how to ascertain which ladies might be amenable to what you're seeking and at what point we will disclose your requirements. Unless… I suppose we could just make your requirements known. Then, only interested ladies would encourage your attentions."

He narrowed his eyes. "What do you mean by making my requirements known? Do you plan to take out an advertisement in the local newspaper?" He flashed a smile, and she realized he was jesting.

"I know enough people in Marrywell." Several

ladies came to mind. "I could simply spread the information about."

"Gossip, you mean."

Rebecca wrinkled her nose. "That sounds unsavory, but yes. It would be expedient."

"Let me think on that."

"As you wish. We've time to decide." She desperately wanted to ask him why he didn't want to fall in love, but suspected she knew. His wife had died, and, unlike Rebecca, he'd mourned his spouse's death. It might be that he simply didn't want to love again. Objectively, Rebecca could understand that, but realistically, she could not. As someone who'd grown up without love and married without love, she wanted that more than anything. And if she couldn't have it for herself, she would help others to find it.

Then what was she doing with Creslow?

If you want to be a matchmaker, you must make the match for which you were hired.

She could do that. She must. Hopefully, she wouldn't regret it.

CHAPTER 4

*L*ate the following morning, Mrs. Sweet took Nash on a tour of Marrywell. He was delighted by how many people remembered her and basked in the warmth of her expression each time she encountered someone she knew.

What did not delight him was how everyone reacted to meeting him. Once they heard he was a marquess and that he was in search of a bride, they universally declared that he would be the most popular gentleman in town, just as Mrs. Thomason had done.

Nash worried he would be overrun at tomorrow's welcome reception. He considered what Mrs. Sweet had suggested, that he make it known he was not looking for a love match. However, if he did that, the news would surely travel back to London, and he wasn't enthused about his personal life being so public, for that would raise questions he didn't want to hear, let alone answer.

Dammit, this was proving more difficult than he'd anticipated.

As they walked along the High Street toward the botanical gardens, Mrs. Sweet nodded toward a bakery as they passed. "They make the best ginger cakes, if you're ever in need of one."

"I shall keep that in mind. Have you given any thought to how we might proceed without making my marchioness requirements known?"

"I have," she said slowly. "That will be more challenging, but you could limit your dancing and pay attention only to ladies with whom you sense a potential physical compatibility. You'll just need to be... discerning." She lifted her shoulder in a faint shrug. "I'm still thinking about possible strategies."

He sensed a bit of nervousness from her. "I have every confidence in you."

She looked over at him, gratitude in her eyes. "Thank you. I will do my best to see you settled."

Settled. He doubted he would ever feel that way, not after his sad, short marriage. He supposed he saw everything as temporary. And that was *un*settling.

Mrs. Sweet gestured in front of them. "This is Garden Street. On the opposite corner—over there— are the assembly rooms." She indicated a large building with a Palladian front, which faced Garden Street.

They crossed the street and walked through the gate into the gardens, following the path through manicured lawn and lush flowerbeds. Nash pointed to a faux temple up ahead. "Is that a folly?"

"Yes, there are several throughout the gardens."

"It *is* Rebecca Webster!" Yet another resident rushed toward Mrs. Sweet, smiling. The woman looked to be about the same age as Mrs. Sweet, perhaps a year or two older. "Begging your pardon, you are Mrs. Sweet now, of course."

Mrs. Sweet greeted the woman with a wide smile of her own. "How are you, Daisy?"

"Well, thank you. You look *very* well." Daisy cast a suggestive glance toward Nash.

"I must introduce the Marquess of Creslow," Mrs. Sweet said. "I am helping him find a match during the festival."

Daisy gave him a brief curtsey. "Pleased to meet you, my lord." She looked back to Mrs. Sweet. "Are you a matchmaker now? I was sorry to hear about Mr. Sweet. We missed you at Leah and Phin's wedding last year." Daisy's blue eyes rounded. "Can you believe she's the blooming *May Queen*?" She laughed with glee.

Mrs. Sweet didn't laugh with her. Indeed, she looked surprised. "Is she? I didn't realize."

Nash wanted to know who Leah and Phin were.

"Mama! Mama!" Three children came running toward them from behind Daisy.

The woman turned. "You finally caught up with me, then, did you?"

"Papa said we had to," the oldest, a girl, said. She held the hand of the youngest, a boy.

The middle child, another boy, moved to take his mother's hand. "We helped him all we could."

Daisy stroked the boy's cheek with a tender smile. "I'm sure you did." She turned back to Nash and Mrs. Sweet. "These are my children. My husband is a brewer. He's setting up in the brewer's field, and we brought him some luncheon."

"I came to help!" the boy said, proudly swinging his mother's hand.

The daughter swept the younger boy, who looked to be about three years old, into her arms. "James is tired, Mama."

"Yes, let's get him home." Daisy gave Mrs. Sweet a warm smile. "It's wonderful to see you. I hope you'll be staying longer than the festival. It's such a busy time, and I'd hope we'll have time to visit."

"I'm not sure, but yes, it would be lovely." Mrs.

Sweet's gaze moved over the children. "Your family is beautiful."

"Thank you." Daisy went to take the youngest in her arms and delivered the other boy's hand to his sister. "Come on now, you lot."

They walked on toward the gate.

Nash pivoted toward Mrs. Sweet. "You have been missed here in Marrywell. Why did you leave?"

"I met my husband at the festival nine years ago. He proposed, and we wed here in Marrywell after the banns were read. Then, I went to live with him in Leighton Buzzard."

"That's how my cousin knows you."

Mrs. Sweet started walking once more, and Nash fell in beside her. "My former husband's aunt is a dear friend of Lady Philpott."

"Ah, yes, Mrs. St. James. I've met her on several occasions. I want to say I'm surprised I haven't met you before last September, but I only visit my cousin once a year at most—at her annual house party. You can't have been at any of the ones I attended, for I am certain I would have remembered you." There was no question about that. From her brilliant red hair to the freckles dotting the bridge of her nose to the plump swell of her lower lip, her face was forever imprinted on his mind.

"Last year was the first time I was invited. Aunt Jennet—my husband's aunt—arranged for me to join her."

They were quiet for several steps before he asked, "Do you miss Marrywell?"

She looked straight ahead as they walked. "I didn't."

"Who are Leah and Phin? Are they people you missed?" Nash wondered if they were family.

It took her a long moment to answer. Her neck flushed pink above the edge of her spencer.

"Phineas Radford owns the botanical gardens. His family is one of the oldest in Marrywell. Leah is my sister."

Her sister was the May Queen? And she hadn't known?

She hadn't visited in nearly a decade. And she'd just said she hadn't missed her home.

Nash was most curious about what had driven Mrs. Sweet from Marrywell. For it seemed that was what had happened. Had she married to get away? Or was it simply that her husband had been a terrible brute and not allowed her to visit? If that were the case, Nash would have thought she would have returned after his death.

"Come, I'll show you the brewer's field," she said with an overbright smile, as if she were trying to push thoughts of her sister away. Well, he would let her. For now.

"That would be delightful." He returned her smile. "Lead the way."

It wasn't a long walk, and as they neared a tall hedge, she indicated that it surrounded the brewer's field. "It offers a shield for when things become raucous."

Nash wondered if it could rival a London public house. Before he could ask, however, a couple came through the opening in the hedge, from the brewer's field. He was tall, with auburn hair topped with what looked like a farmer's hat and in his middle twenties. She was of a similar age, with blonde curls framing her face beneath the brim of her hat. The rounding of her belly was unmistakable—the woman was with child.

A sharp intake of breath came from Mrs. Sweet. Nash turned his head to see her face had paled. This *had* to be Leah and Phin.

Except, looking back to the woman, Nash didn't

see a family resemblance between her and Mrs. Sweet. Perhaps he was wrong.

"Good afternoon, Rebecca," the blonde woman said.

"Good afternoon, Leah," Mrs. Sweet responded, her voice thin.

For some reason, Nash moved closer to his matchmaker in case she needed support. He'd no idea what was causing her distress, but he meant to be there for her whether she wanted him to or not.

~

*R*ebecca managed to take a breath as the shock of seeing Leah after so long gripped her. And the surprise didn't come from how different Leah looked from the last time they'd seen each other. They'd both been much younger, and now Leah was apparently expecting a child.

Seeing Leah brought all Rebecca's regret and guilt to the surface, but it had been simmering very close to that since she'd arrived in Marrywell the day before. One of the reasons she'd suggested Creslow seek his match at the festival was so she could face her past. Now that she was doing that, Rebecca wondered why she'd thought it was a good idea at all.

She hadn't expected to just run into them like this. She'd wanted to plan, to prepare. Could she, though? Was there really any way for her to see her family and not feel a mix of dread and anxiety?

"You look well," Leah said, appearing unaffected by this surprise meeting. Or perhaps she was just better at hiding things.

"Thank you," Rebecca said, grasping at the words and forcing them from her lips. "As do you. Congratulations." She dipped her gaze to Leah's swollen belly.

"Thank you. We'll be welcoming the baby in June."

So soon. Rebecca hated that she felt a pang of envy. Leah deserved every happiness. In fact, Rebecca deserved the opposite. She often wondered if that was why her marriage had turned out so poorly and she had no children. It was the price she paid for her treatment of Leah when they were young.

Feeling suddenly queasy, Rebecca transferred her attention to Phin, thinking he would be easier to address. He looked like such a man now, but of course he would after nearly a decade. "You also appear well, Phin."

Phin gave her a warm smile. "It's lovely to see you, Rebecca." He glanced toward Creslow, and Rebecca realized she'd been remiss in not introducing him.

She turned slightly toward him, and her arm grazed his. He'd moved closer, but she hadn't noticed. Now she did. His proximity was a surprisingly welcome support. "Allow me to present my employer, the Marquess of Creslow."

"Your employer?" Leah asked.

"Mrs. Sweet is my matchmaker," Creslow said with an especially disarming smile.

"How splendid." Leah's gaze met Rebecca's once more. "I didn't know you'd taken on a new occupation, nor that you would be visiting Marrywell."

"It happened rather quickly."

Leah's gaze softened, and Rebecca wished she could flee. She didn't want her sister's kindness or her understanding. There were too many things Rebecca needed to say first. But Rebecca didn't even know where to begin. Furthermore, she certainly wasn't going to say *anything* in front of the marquess. Or Phin. This was between Rebecca and her younger sister.

"Well, I'm glad you've come," Leah said. "We missed you at the wedding last year, though we understood why you couldn't come."

"Because I was in mourning," Rebecca murmured. She'd sent a brief letter of congratulations.

There was a beat of silence, and to Rebecca, it felt uncomfortable. But then this entire encounter made her want to run away from Marrywell and never return.

She hadn't thought this through. Part of her wanted to reconcile with Leah and the rest of her family, especially now that their mother was no longer there. But part of her also didn't want to face the pain.

She was such a coward.

Creslow, bless him, ended the quiet. "I understand you are the May Queen," he said jovially to Leah.

"Yes, and Phin is the May King, of course."

Phin waved his hand and smiled. "Bah, the attention is always on the ladies—the queen and her court. Are you looking forward to our festival, my lord?"

"Creslow, if you please. I'm certainly intrigued. Particularly by the brewer's field." He looked past Leah and Phin.

"Ah, yes. This is a popular destination," Phin said. He leaned forward and gave Creslow a conspiratorial nod. "If you come back later this evening, they'll be pouring ale for one another. Honestly, it's usually the most entertaining night to be in the brewer's field, as you get to listen to them talk about their craft. Until they're too stewed to do so." He laughed. "Alas, I am often so busy with last-minute tasks that I am not able to join them for long."

"Tonight is different, however," Leah said with a note of pride. "This year, we have more help, and the gardens are ready to welcome everyone to the festival tomorrow evening for the crowning ceremony and the opening of the labyrinth." She looked to Rebecca. "In fact, you should join us for dinner this evening. That way, we can have time to visit before the festival overwhelms us."

Leah couldn't possibly want Rebecca under her roof. Why was she being so nice?

Because she was happy. She'd married the man she'd been besotted with since childhood—something most people didn't know, but that Rebecca had puzzled out the year before she'd wed Horatio.

Rebecca smiled faintly. "As much as I would enjoy that, I'm afraid I must spend the evening with the marquess. We've much to do to prepare for the week ahead."

"He should join us too," Phin said, looking toward Creslow. "It would be our pleasure to invite you to Radford Grange."

"I'd be delighted," Nash said. "If you're sure it isn't an imposition."

"Not at all," Leah assured him.

Rebecca couldn't decline now without arousing everyone's curiosity.

"It's settled, then." Leah's entire countenance lit with anticipation. "We'll see you at six."

"We should be on our way." Phin put his hand on Leah's back. "Still much to do before tomorrow."

They took their leave. Rebecca felt her body start to shake. Moving away from Creslow, she clasped her hands together and stiffened her spine until she regained control.

"Are you all right?" he asked, following her to where she'd stepped, out of the path of the entrance to the brewer's field.

Summoning another weak smile, she faced him. "Quite. I was merely surprised to see my sister. I'm looking forward to later." Only, she wasn't. She couldn't very well spend time over dinner with Leah without saying something about the past. But how did one apologize for remaining silent while their mother had treated Leah so cruelly?

"Are you sure you don't mind if I come along?" He regarded her with deep concern. "I don't have to if that's what you'd prefer."

He'd sensed Rebecca's discomfort. There was curiosity in his gaze as well as kindness. She didn't want to deal with either. "Do you mind if we return to the inn?"

"Not at all. Shall we return the way we came?"

"That would be simplest." She started walking along the path, and he moved alongside her.

They'd nearly reached the gate when he finally said, "Forgive me if I'm being intrusive, but you seem unsettled. I should like to help if I may."

This would not do. Rebecca stopped abruptly and pivoted toward him. "You *are* being intrusive, and I would like you not to be. I regret that my personal life has intruded on our professional association."

He'd faced her when she'd stopped. "There's no need," he said quickly. "I would actually like if we could be friends as well as business associates."

Rebecca didn't want his concern. She didn't *deserve* it, especially about this. "Our relationship must remain professional."

"There is nothing saying so." Edging closer, the marquess lifted his hand as if he meant to touch her. Rebecca recoiled.

"Please don't," she said sharply. "There can't be a repeat of what happened at Clipstone Hedge. This is a business arrangement."

He exhaled. "All right. I would like to make one final comment about that evening, if I may. No, I'm going to do it anyway." His gaze locked with hers, and he spoke in a soft, sensual tone that stirred a keen yearning inside her. "I regret not spending the night with you. I do hope you'll find someone else to finish what we started—you deserve that after the husband you had."

"You shouldn't say such things." Now she wanted to be proper? After what she'd allowed him to do to her in that library? Her body heated.

"I will still hope we can be friends," he said. "When you find me a bride, perhaps I can repay the favor by finding you a lover."

Her breath caught when he spoke that last word. Willing her ardor to cool, she lifted her chin. "You hired me to find you a bride. This is not a *favor*."

He inclined his head, his eyes sparkling in the afternoon sun. "Fair enough. Though, I didn't mean to imply I wouldn't still pay you. I'd still be glad to help —in any way you deem necessary. For you see, Mrs. Sweet, whether you like it or not, I think we are friends. Only a friend will be able to ensure I don't choose a poor marchioness."

Rebecca wasn't even certain she'd be able to do that given his stringent requirements. But she was determined to do her best. "Just so long as you accept that is all we will be. Agreed?"

He nodded once. "Agreed."

"No more smiling at me in a charming manner. Understand?"

He started to smile and quickly quashed the expression, pressing his lips together so they disappeared. "As you wish."

It wasn't really what she wished. But it was the way it had to be.

CHAPTER 5

*S*itting beside Creslow in his elegant coach on the way to Radford Grange, Rebecca reconsidered her decision to attend dinner for what was probably the hundredth time. She'd considered asking the marquess not to come, but in the end, she was a coward because she didn't want to face this alone.

Did that make Creslow what he purported to be—her friend? She supposed it made him something. She just needed to ensure that whatever their relationship, it wouldn't interfere with the primary objective of finding him a marchioness.

Though his coach was large, she could still feel his body heat beside her on the seat they shared. He wasn't touching her, but the notion that he could if the coach hit a rut and they jostled together was enough to make the air crackle with anticipation.

Radford Grange was about three miles by road, and it adjoined the far edge of the botanical gardens from the town. Rebecca glimpsed the manor house from the window on her side of the coach. "There it is."

Creslow leaned slightly over her to see it. His scent of sandalwood filled her nostrils, and she felt an instant pulse of arousal. She pressed herself back against the squab lest they come into contact with one another.

Moving back, he adjusted his coat. "Looks as though it was built in the seventeenth century. Or is that a new façade?"

"I'm not sure, but I would guess it's the latter. I believe the original building dates to the fifteenth century. I know it's been enlarged and refurbished many times since then."

"I can imagine. I confess I'm fascinated by architecture. My family's pile was built in 1690 and underwent a refurbishment about fifty years ago. I'd like to add a conservatory."

Rebecca was grateful for a topic of conversation that wasn't personal and seized it. "Do you spend a great deal of time there?"

"No. Not since… I'm typically in London or traveling about."

"Not since your wife passed away?" Rebecca hoped he might answer, but he didn't even look in her direction. "Perhaps when you add a conservatory, you will," she added as the coach made its way up the drive toward the manor house.

The coach came to a stop, and the marquess stepped out to help Rebecca down. She ignored the jolt of delight that shot up her arm when she put her hand in his and removed herself from his grasp as soon as possible.

The elderly butler, who moved at a snail's pace, admitted them and showed them to the drawing room. Rebecca had only visited Radford Grange a handful of times in her youth, and she vaguely remembered the butler had been old then.

Leah rose from a chair as they entered. "Welcome to Radford Grange."

Rebecca glanced toward the marquess to see how

he'd respond. He'd been stiff and silent since she'd mentioned his wife's death in the coach.

Creslow smiled warmly, all evidence of his upset now gone, and bowed. "Thank you. Please, sit back down."

"Yes, do," Phin said, giving Leah a pointed look. He turned to Rebecca and Creslow. "She was very busy today, and while the babe isn't yet due for several more weeks, I keep telling her she should get her rest now."

Rebecca could hardly believe her sister lived in this grand house and was married to a man she adored with a baby on the way. This was everything she deserved, and yet it was vastly different from what any of them had expected when Leah had departed Marrywell to become a lady's companion. Rebecca had already left by then herself, but her brother's wife had written to tell her about it.

"You look very happy," Rebecca said tentatively. "I'm so pleased for you." There, she'd said something, at least. But it wasn't the apology Leah deserved. As if a simple apology could ever compensate for the cruelty Leah had endured, and which Rebecca and her siblings had been forced to silently witness.

Leah gave her a warm smile. "I am, thank you."

"Tell me about your house," Creslow said, unwittingly easing Rebecca's anxiety by redirecting the conversation to something...safe. "Mrs. Sweet tells me it dates to the fifteenth century, but the façade is clearly newer."

Phin moved toward him, his pale features animated. "This house has been extended more times than I can count. The staircase hall is really all that's left of that original building, and the stairs have been rebuilt. Still, you get a distinctly medieval sensibility from that room."

Creslow nodded with interest. "Perhaps I can

have a tour another time. What of the botanical gardens? I understand you own and oversee those as well."

"Indeed. My grandfather opened them to the people of Marrywell for their use. The part nearest town, along Garden Street, with the dais, has been used for the matchmaking festival for over a hundred years. Grandpapa wanted to create a space where the festival could grow and encourage more activities, even beyond matchmaking."

"What do you mean?" Creslow asked. "I thought for this next week, all of Marrywell was about making matches."

Phin chuckled, but it was Leah who answered. "That is the primary objective, but with the addition of the brewer's field and a variety of competitions and amusements, the festival now involves a great many people who aren't seeking a match. The pudding competition draws cooks from all over the district."

Rebecca blinked at her sister. "Ten years ago, that was less a competition and more an excuse to overindulge in excellent puddings."

"It still is," Phin said, grinning.

"Sounds delightful to me." Creslow turned his head to Rebecca. "I hope this is part of your plan of activities."

He expected her to have a plan of activities? The better question was perhaps why she didn't already. "Yes. We can review the specific events later. Or tomorrow morning."

"How wonderful that Rebecca is your matchmaker," Leah said. "I'm confident she will find the perfect bride for you."

Rebecca tensed. She didn't deserve Leah's kindness. But perhaps Leah had simply decided to move on from the past. Given the near perfection of her current situation, why wouldn't she? Or, mayhap she didn't need Rebecca's apology. Anyway, wouldn't anything Rebecca said be too little effort far too late?

The ancient butler shuffled in to announce dinner, and Rebecca accepted yet another reprieve. Was it really a reprieve, though? Just being in Leah's presence was a terrible reminder of a past of which she was ashamed. She either needed to find a way to move past it herself—or finally own up to it.

~

They didn't stay long after dinner. Rebecca could tell that Leah was tired. She'd always been more tired than the rest of them, for their mother would burden her with chores late at night and again early in the morning, rousing her before anyone else in the household. Of course, that wasn't the reason now—she was simply carrying a babe.

Rebecca had tried to be conversational at dinner, but found it difficult to speak past the seemingly ever-present lump in her throat. Thankfully, the gentlemen found plenty to discuss. In fact, Rebecca thought her employer and Phin might have formed a lasting friendship.

"You were quiet this evening," Creslow said from beside her.

"Was I?" She clasped her hands in her lap instead of mentioning how he'd gone silent after she'd asked about his wife.

"I suppose I expected you and your sister to share stories about your childhood in Marrywell or that you'd be lost in conversation with one another since you've been apart so long."

"We weren't particularly close." It wasn't a lie exactly. Rebecca would have liked to have been, but doing so had invited punishment from their mother.

"I find that surprising. Your sister is most engaging, as are you." He turned toward her as if he expected a more...intimate exchange.

Rebecca stiffened and scooted as far as possible to the side of the coach away from him. "You're too curious about my family." If he didn't want to share his past with her, why should she share hers with him?

"I'm curious about *you*. And before you tell me I shouldn't be, that such things are none of my affair, I'll remind you that you're my employee. I need to ensure you're up to snuff."

Frowning, she shot him a quelling glance. "You are shameless."

"I could just talk to your sister."

Rebecca threw up her hands and turned her head toward him. "What is it you want from me?"

"I don't want anything *from* you. I only wish to dispel that dark storm cloud that moves over your head whenever you see your sister, or your family is mentioned."

She wanted to turn away from him, to hide herself in the shame of the past. Better still, she wanted to ask about the dark cloud that hovered over him whenever Rebecca asked about his wife.

Perhaps if she shared something of herself, he'd do the same. Even if he didn't, she couldn't deny the lure of unburdening herself. Closing her eyes briefly, she said, "I was afraid to come back here. To Marrywell."

"Why were you scared?" He sounded so caring, so genuinely concerned. It was no wonder he'd worn her down.

She worried her fingers together, pinching the fingertip of one hand with the thumb and forefinger of the other. "My childhood wasn't happy."

"Why don't you tell me about your family," he encouraged gently.

Summoning her courage, she took a deep breath before starting. "You may have noted that Leah and I don't resemble each other. I take after my mother. Leah takes after our father—and also her mother, who was not the same as mine, or our other siblings. We have an older brother, Barnabas, and an older sister, Meg."

"I see," he murmured.

"We were never allowed to discuss Leah's parentage, but we all knew, of course. Leah was kept separate from us. I shared a chamber with Meg, but Mother made Leah sleep in a small chamber on a pallet. It was a cupboard really, for there was no window."

Rebecca's insides clenched. It had been so long since she'd allowed herself to think about the past to this degree. And she certainly hadn't talked about it. Now, the words spilled forth as if a dam had broken free.

"Leah was treated differently from you because of her parentage?" he asked.

Nodding, Rebecca flattened her hands on her lap. "When I was old enough to realize the inequity—that word is so insufficient to truly describe the difference in how we were treated—I tried to intervene. It was winter, and Leah's room was so cold. I brought her to my bed, to sleep with me because Meg and I had a hearth. When my mother discovered us in the morning, she punished us both. I wasn't allowed supper for a week, and she...well, she was cruel." Rebecca squeezed her fingers together once more.

"Did she hurt you?"

"Yes. It was enough to ensure I never tried to help Leah again. We were all miserable, but none of us so much as Leah. Seeing her now...she's so happy." A humiliating sob escaped Rebecca's lips, and she clapped her hand over her mouth.

Creslow took her free hand in his. The warmth and comfort helped ease the tension curling through Rebecca's body. She worked to take a breath, trying to calm herself before she dissolved into a puddle of tears.

His grip was gentle, his gaze kind. "I'm not quite sure if these are glad tears or sad tears. I would say the latter, but you mentioned your sister's happiness, so I'm not entirely certain."

Rebecca sniffed. "I am glad for her—so very glad. But I am sad that I wasn't a good sister to her. She deserved better."

"She didn't seem to think so," he said softly. "I saw a woman who was pleased to see her sister, who enjoyed her company this evening and looked forward to the next time you would be together."

As they'd left, Leah had said she hoped to see them at the welcome reception and crowning ceremony tomorrow. "She was just being polite," Rebecca said.

"That wasn't my impression." He took a breath, his hand still clasping hers. Rebecca was grateful for his touch. "Forgive me for opining, but I do not think your sister bears you ill will, nor is she holding a grudge. She seems quite happy. Perhaps you simply need to let the past rest and look to the future."

"I have to say something to her—to at least acknowledge what happened." Rebecca shook her head. She didn't know what to do with a sister who didn't hate her or at least blame her for her miserable childhood. "She was driven from Marrywell. From the man she loved. But at least she found him again and things turned out at they should."

"It seems as though you were also driven from Marrywell," he observed quietly. "You were very young when you wed, were you not?"

"Nineteen."

"And did you fall madly in love with him? That is not my impression based on what you've shared of your marriage, but perhaps the union started better than it ended."

"It did not, and I did not fall in love with him, madly or otherwise. It was my first festival as a marriageable young lady, and I was eager to wed and get away. That Horatio lived far from Marrywell was an advantage I leapt at."

"Then you *were* driven away too."

Rebecca sucked in a breath. She *had* been driven away. By her mother. And by her guilt. "I just needed to leave Black Sheep Farm," she whispered. "But I didn't *need* to get away, not like Leah did."

"I would urge you to not look back at the past and think of what you should have done. You are far wiser now than you were then. I'm sure you'll find a way to use that to do whatever you feel is necessary. Whatever guilt you harbor, however, is yours, and your sister doesn't seem to expect anything from you."

Rebecca wiped her free hand over her eyes and looked at him. "Why am I such a coward about this?"

He smiled. "You aren't. You've a heart full of love, and a mind full of regret. I find it's best to empty the latter, for it will only weigh you down."

Rebecca knew he was right. It was past time for her to talk to Leah, to say everything she should have done more than a decade before. "How did *you* get so wise?"

Laughing softly, he shrugged. "I don't think I am, but I have two younger sisters, and I think siblings are worth fighting for. I also know something of pain and raising oneself out of it." He lifted her hand to his lips and pressed a kiss to the back. Though she wore gloves, she felt the press of his flesh as if her hand were bare.

"You shouldn't do that." Her voice was low and husky, her body tingling with arousal despite her recent emotional upheaval. Or perhaps because of it. She felt vulnerable. Raw. Eager for connection with someone.

With him.

"I vow that whatever happens in the carriage stays in the carriage." His eyes glimmered with promise.

"We could just pretend it never happened?"

"We could."

Then they could kiss and act as if they hadn't. Or he could caress her as he had in the library. Or she could caress him as she'd hoped to do and dreamed of doing since.

The coach pulled to a stop at the inn. Disappointment unfurled inside her. She withdrew her hand from his grasp. "I'll keep that in mind. Thank you for your counsel. I suppose I must now submit to your friendship."

He laughed, more loudly than before. "Then this has been a most beneficial excursion." He climbed out of the coach and helped her to the ground. "I look forward to our next trip in the carriage. Who knows what will happen?"

Rebecca could hope that he might share some of himself as she had done. Perhaps he'd expand on what he meant about raising himself out of pain.

It was possible he was referring to something more physical happening between them, but they both knew that couldn't happen. They could share confidences and build on their friendship.

And that was all.

CHAPTER 6

*M*rs. Sweet had requested they break
their fast together this morning so that
they could plan for the day's events. Nash didn't care
why they would eat together, just that he got to
spend more time with the fascinating and deeply alluring matchmaker.

Her revelations to him in the coach the previous
night had allowed him to see a part of her that he
suspected she rarely, if ever, shared. He felt humbled
and privileged, but also more curious than ever. He
also felt an increasing desire that went beyond simple
physical arousal. The more he learned of her, the
more he wanted to know—and to help.

The pain of her childhood and what had happened to her sister was so real to him. Nash knew
what it was like to blame oneself. He'd done that for a
long time after his wife had become ill, just a few
months into their marriage. Despite spending the
next year tending to her as the cancer overtook her
body, he still questioned what more he could have
done. Not necessarily to lengthen her life—though he
sometimes thought of that too—but to make her
more comfortable, especially near the end.

"Good morning," Mrs. Sweet said as she arrived at their table in the common room.

Nash rose and held her chair, glad that her arrival would put an end to his maudlin thoughts. He worked hard to keep them at bay. "Good morning. I trust you slept well."

"Quite, thank you."

He could not say the same, for he'd been kept awake thinking of her. Of her troubles and of future trips in his coach. He found himself wondering where they could go when it seemed everything to do with the festival was within walking distance.

"Are you ready to discuss our plan for finding you a marchioness?" she asked.

"I suppose I must be since that is our objective this week. Have you obtained sufficient information about me to do what is necessary?"

"I think so. Before we continue, what have you decided about sharing your requirements? Do you want to make them widely known or share them with ladies as you see fit?"

Every time he thought about it, he imagined people asking him why he wouldn't marry for love. He realized it was a very odd demand, and he couldn't answer with the truth. There was no chance he would discuss his wife or his grief. That was the whole point of avoiding love, so he could leave the pain where it belonged—in the past.

"I will be most comfortable with the latter plan. If it becomes gossip, people will want to know why I have these requirements, and I refuse to answer any such queries."

"Even when your matchmaker asks," she murmured.

Nash snapped his gaze toward her as irritation flashed through him. But she was within her rights to be curious and expect an explanation. Except it wouldn't help her find him a wife. "It doesn't signify."

"I doubt your future wife would agree. What of honesty and trust in a marriage? Shouldn't your bride know whom she's marrying?"

He heard the sharpness in her tone and recognized that she'd been duped by her cad of a husband. "I have loved before and don't think I can do so again," he said quickly.

"Then perhaps it's better to say that you *may* not love your bride instead of demanding the emotion can't have a place in your union."

"No." He suddenly felt as if he were drowning. He struggled to breathe. Clenching his jaw, he willed himself to push the panicked thoughts away. After a moment, he managed a semideep breath and looked her directly in the eye. "I will not fall in love, and I will not marry anyone who expects it of me. Are we clear on that?"

She pressed her lips together so that they nearly vanished. "Perfectly."

Thankfully, Mrs. Thomason interrupted them by bringing their breakfast of ham and buns, as well as tea. She poured their cups and departed.

They ate in silence for a moment, and Nash felt like a boor. But he couldn't change who he was or what he wanted. Or what he *didn't* want. Hopefully, he hadn't frightened her away.

Mrs. Sweet stirred her tea as she cast him a look of uncertainty. "Today, I wish to observe you with as many potential brides as possible. And I want you to tell me which ones meet your... requirements of attraction."

"At what point will we determine if they are interested in what I'm offering?"

A slight grimace creased her beautiful features. "I'm not yet sure, but we have to start somewhere.

My hope is that today at the reception and tonight at the welcome ball, we'll both be able to make assessments. You'll determine which ladies are of interest to you, and I'll ascertain whether they are open to the arrangement you desire."

Desire. At the moment, he felt that for precisely one woman, and she was seated across from him.

He took a moment to eat some ham and wash it down with tea. "And what of the magic?"

She'd also busied herself with eating a bun, and now her brows shot up. "Magic?"

"Whatever it is that you detect between two people that makes you think they'll suit."

"Well, this is a different sort of match," she said slowly. "I don't think my expertise—if that's what you want to call it—will be particularly helpful."

He reached for one of the small buns on his plate, thinking that he'd given her an extremely challenging assignment. "How will you determine if a lady is even interested in my arrangement?"

"Leave that to me." She took a bite of ham.

He watched her as he chewed on his bun. Did she even know? "I might wonder if you've worked out that part yet. Do let me know if I can be of assistance."

"I had considered how you could help, and I've an idea. However, I'm not sure you'll want to do it." She took a breath before continuing, her gaze meeting his. "You may want to be less...charming than usual."

Nash was swallowing a mouthful of sweet bun as laughter jumped up his throat. He coughed and took a drink of tea. "Why?"

She lifted a shoulder. "You don't want anyone to fall in love with you. Perhaps you should also mess your hair or scuff your boots."

"I'm too charming and too attractive?"

Nodding, she added, "You could also stop smiling. Yes, that might help."

He couldn't stop the shout of laughter that leapt from him. Or the thread of heat her words stoked. She must find him charming and attractive. And that made him a little giddy.

It took a few minutes, but Nash schooled his features into a scowl and jutted his chin out. "How's this?"

"Try grunting."

He made a wholly primal sound in his throat.

She giggled. "That may be a trifle too much."

"I daresay I'm going to confuse everyone. If they've heard of my reputation, they will expect a rakish cavalier. Instead, they'll encounter a brooding stoic."

She shook her head. "Don't brood. Too many young ladies find that attractive. Blame gothic love stories. And Lord Byron."

Nash sniggered. "You are probably right. I'll just scowl and ask the valet to refrain from polishing my boots, then."

"I don't suppose you own any ugly waistcoats? Something in puce or drab brown?" A wicked smile curled her lips, and Nash was utterly rapt. He would do whatever she suggested next. Immediately. "Perhaps you could ask the valet to adjust your coat so that it doesn't fit properly."

"I want *someone* to find me attractive," he said with a laugh.

"Well, I highly doubt we'll convince everyone that you aren't. And those are the ones who will likely be open to your arrangement."

They continued eating for another few minutes. He sat back as he finished the last of his ham. "It seems as though we have a plan."

"Indeed. I am most optimistic."

He wanted to ask her about last night, mostly to see if she was feeling any better about her sister. "I'm glad to hear it. I hope that extends to all aspects of your visit to Marrywell."

She jerked her gaze up from her plate. "If you're referring to my family, I'd rather not discuss that just now. I'm focused on my job. On *you*."

Nash could not argue with that. In fact, he'd be thrilled to have her entirely focused on him. And not as his matchmaker.

How in the hell was he going to determine if any of the ladies at the festival were attractive to him when he'd already found one who was completely alluring in every way?

Perhaps he should postpone this bloody match-making plan and instead pursue what he really wanted right now—a love affair with his match-maker. Spending the next week closeted at the Buck and Maiden with Mrs. Sweet sounded ideal.

She set her teacup down, the clack interrupting his terribly wayward thoughts. "We will depart for the reception at three. I'll meet you down here." She was already on her feet before he managed to launch himself from the chair.

"Excellent. I'm looking forward to it."

And his anticipation had absolutely nothing to do with finding a bride.

~

*R*ebecca stood in the common room awaiting Creslow's arrival. She'd lied to him earlier when she'd told him she'd slept well. In actuality, she'd failed to find sleep for some time, which wasn't unusual for her. However, in this case, it was entirely because she kept thinking of the evening with Leah. It was difficult to reconcile the joy she felt at seeing her sister's happiness with the guilt that haunted Rebecca from the past. She'd finally fallen asleep after realizing that the guilt was *her* problem, and if Leah could manage to move on, Rebecca needed to as well.

The very next time she saw her sister, Rebecca would tell her how sorry she was and how much she loved her. And how proud she was to call her sister.

At the sound of footfalls on the stairs, Rebecca turned. The marquess appeared, carrying his hat as he descended. He looked...different. While they'd discussed that, she hadn't quite expected him to do anything.

His sable hair was combed severely to the side with an excess of pomade. He looked like a youth trying to emulate his father's style. His very simply tied cravat was an odd color—a dull yellow—that didn't particularly match his amber-colored waistcoat. And he wore a dark blue jacket with brown breeches. The entire ensemble just looked...off. As a final touch, his boots had not been polished.

"Smile," she said.

"You told me not to."

"I want to see if you've blackened your teeth."

A loud guffaw erupted from him, and he grinned. "As you can see, I did not, but I'm sure I can get some soot from the hearth over there—"

"No!" She had to grab his sleeve, for he was already pivoting in that direction. "You've done enough. You don't look at all dashing."

He did to her, of course. Because he still smelled of sandalwood, and she would never be able to look at him without thinking of him kissing her, touching her, arousing her beyond reason. She released him before she did something utterly foolish, like draw him close to her.

"Are you certain the soot wouldn't help? I also

considered asking Martin—the splendid valet—to spill tea on my cravat, but we ran out of time."

"You are sufficiently less attractive. Let us be on our way. It looks as though it may rain."

"Should we take the coach?" he asked, sounding hopeful. Was he thinking of last night? About when he'd said that whatever happened in the carriage stayed in the carriage?

"We don't have time." She moved to the door, and he hastened to open it for her.

They walked to the street, then turned toward the High Street. She looked at him from the side of her eye and stopped short.

She turned toward him. "Is your jacket missing buttons?"

"Yes," he answered proudly.

"I didn't think you'd take this plan so…seriously."

"This is serious business. I can't have ladies swooning at the sight of me." His lips quivered, and she suspected he was trying not to laugh.

"I don't think we discussed the possibility of that happening."

"Not that specifically, but you were right in that I should dissuade anyone from falling in love with me. It's better if they see me as a business proposition. An alignment of like interests."

"In your current state, you are going to attract someone whose interests are eccentric clothing and overdone hairstyles. Not that there is anything wrong with those things, but I don't think that's who you are. Or at least not who your valet allows you to be."

"You are correct," Creslow responded as they turned onto the High Street. "I wouldn't know eccentric clothing if that was all that was in my dressing chamber. I instructed Martin to put together a displeasing ensemble."

"And the hair?" Rebecca asked.

"Also Martin's handiwork. I shudder to think what my valet would say if he saw me today."

Rebecca smiled. "Where is your valet?"

"In London caring for his mother. She took ill just before we left, and I knew he would be concerned for her."

"You allowed him to stay with her?" She already knew the answer of course, and it warmed her. How a man treated those who worked for him said a great deal about his character. "That was kind of you. Especially since you readily admit you wouldn't know how to dress yourself."

He barked out a laugh. "That is not at all what I said. But you may have a point."

Rebecca glanced up at the darkening sky. "We'd better hurry before we're caught in a downpour."

They fortunately arrived at the assembly rooms as dry as when they'd left the inn. A page took their hats and Rebecca's pelisse.

She looked over at Creslow. "Are you ready to implement our plan?"

"As I will ever be." He escorted her into the ballroom, where people were milling about. "What's the point of this reception again? Particularly when everyone will gather for a ball tonight?"

"The May Queen needs an opportunity to select her court before tonight's crowning ceremony. Years ago, when there wasn't a reception, she had to make her selections only shortly after meeting the young ladies in attendance. Often, she wasn't even able to meet all of them. The council felt this was unfair."

"The council?"

"The Marrywellers who organize and oversee the festival every year."

"Are these people elected?"

Rebecca thought of the women who clung to their

positions of power year after year and laughed. "Hardly. Once someone maneuvers their way onto the council, they rarely ever leave."

"I see. Did you ever want to be on this council?"

"I never considered it, actually. My sister and I were far too concerned with whether we would be selected as a maiden fair. And if so, if we could manage to then be voted May Queen."

"And look at your sister now," he said with a soft laugh. "She *is* the May Queen."

"Oh, not that sister." Rebecca had been doing well with her plan to move on from the past, but there were always going to be painful reminders of how they'd left Leah out. "That was me and Meg, my older sister," she said quietly. "She doesn't live in Marrywell. She married and left town the year before me."

"I didn't mean to dredge up things you'd rather forget. My apologies."

Rebecca took a deep breath and squared her shoulders. "It's fine. Indeed, after last night, I realize I need to speak with Leah as soon as possible. Perhaps then, I can move on as she seems to have done. And yet, I hate to trouble her when she seems quite happy. This is my problem, not hers."

"I know I only spent one evening with the two of you, but I daresay she would want you to be happy too." He'd already told her as much last night, but she was glad to hear it again. It bolstered her confidence.

"Thank you. Now, let us focus on the matter at hand—meeting as many potential brides as possible."

He gave her a lopsided smile that made her knees turn to water. "After you."

"Don't do that," she reminded him.

"I shouldn't be polite?"

"Polite is fine. Attractive smiles are not."

Instantly, he smashed his mouth into a frown. "Yes, ma'am."

⁕ They spent the next hour engaging with as many people as possible. Rebecca saw many familiar faces, including her sister, who was also making her way about the room, which was of course her duty as the May Queen. This reception would not be the appropriate place for Rebecca to say what she wanted, and she found she was disappointed instead of relieved.

At one point, she became separated from Creslow, but after about five minutes, he found his way back to her. His brow furrowed slightly as he regarded her. "Do you need a respite? I did. I'm afraid I had to step away and reclaim my energy."

In fact, she was feeling somewhat fatigued. "I should have thought of that."

He waved his hand. "Don't trouble yourself. If you'd like to step out to the sculpture garden, it's most pleasant."

"It's not raining?" she asked.

"Not yet. You'd best hurry."

"Thank you." Rebecca hastened to the garden and took several gulps of fresh spring air. Immediately, she felt restored.

Before returning to the ballroom, she walked to a sculpture she remembered from her youth. It was the goddess Aphrodite, but she wore a wide hooped skirt as if she were a London courtier. She'd looked so elegant and beautiful to Rebecca when she'd been young. She'd stared at the statue and dreamt of being like her, living in a place far from Marrywell. No, that wasn't right—far from Black Sheep Farm.

"This was always my favorite statue."

Rebecca swung about to see her sister Leah standing a few feet away. Her blonde hair was piled atop her head with flowers, which denoted her as the May Queen since she hadn't yet received her crown.

"Mine too," Rebecca said, her heart suddenly thudding against her ribs.

Leah walked toward her. "Seems like we should have known that about one another."

Yes, it did. A hundred responses flitted through Rebecca's head. Without thinking, she said, "I wish we'd been closer."

"I understand why we weren't." Leah stood beside Rebecca, her gaze on the statue.

Rebecca turned toward her sister. "How can you be so understanding?"

"Because I know how horrid she was." Flicking Rebecca a glance, Leah went on, "And still is, but thankfully, she's inflicting her nastiness on others." There was no need to say who "she" was.

"I'm glad she's gone. I don't know if I would have come back to Marrywell if she'd still been here," Rebecca admitted. "I'm surprised you did. When you returned last year, didn't you worry that you'd see her?"

Leah faced Rebecca. "Yes, but my desire to come back—to see Phin—was greater than my fear."

"I'm so glad. That you returned and that you and Phin found happiness together. I know how much you've always cared for him. Well, I suspected anyway."

"Did you?" Leah asked softly. She smiled. "Then, perhaps we were closer than we realized."

"Don't do that," Rebecca whispered, her insides twisting into painful knots. "I don't deserve to feel better about the past."

"Why not? I don't blame you. How could I when I know how awful your mother could be?"

"*I* blame me." Emotion gathered in Rebecca, a tumultuous mix of regret and sadness, with a burst of love too. "I'm so sorry, Leah. I confess I was worried what would happen when we saw each other." She wrung her hands.

"I've forgiven all of you—not that you needed my forgiveness."

Rebecca froze, staring at her. "Even Mother?"

Leah nodded. "Even her." She took Rebecca's hands and gave them a squeeze. "However, that doesn't mean I want to spend time with her," she added with a short laugh. "I would, however, like to do that with you. If you agree."

Could this really be happening? Rebecca had isolated herself from her family and never expected to return to it. "I don't deserve that."

"Nonsense. We all deserve to be happy. I'm sorry your husband died," Leah said softly before releasing Rebecca's hands.

"It's terrible to say, but I'm not. He was selfish, overbearing, and a philanderer. I am happier without him." Just as she'd been happier away from their mother. And why she was working toward a future where she didn't have to listen to other people denigrate her. A future where she could have a home and perhaps love, even if it was just from her family.

Leah regarded her with sympathy. "I had no idea. I don't think anyone else did either. I mean Barn or Meg. Certainly not Father."

"Because I didn't tell them." Rebecca hadn't revealed the state of her marriage or the circumstances of Horatio's death because it was all too humiliating. Furthermore, just as she hadn't felt close to Leah, she hadn't really felt close to any of them. It was as if their family carried a giant weight that constrained them, preventing any sort of strong connection. It was no wonder that three of the four children had moved away.

"You seem to be doing well now, though?" Leah asked hopefully. "Matchmaking for a marquess is no small feat."

"You would know. I was so happy and proud

when I heard a widowed wife of a baronet had hired you as her companion, enabling you to leave Marrywell."

"I was very lucky." Leah's mouth curved into a nostalgic smile. "In many ways, she was the mother I never had. She took very good care of me and introduced me to things I never would have seen or learned."

"She sounds similar to my husband's Aunt Jennet. She's taken me under her wing since Horatio died."

"Oh!" Leah brushed her hand across her cheek. "That was a rather large raindrop. Should we go inside?"

Rebecca looked up. "We seem to have failed to notice an extreme darkening of the sky. Let's hurry. You know how fast and hard it can rain this time of year."

Leah linked her arm through Rebecca's as the rain began to fall. Rebecca hesitated the slightest moment, her body tensing at her sister's touch. But then a raindrop landed on her nose, and she began to move with Leah toward the ballroom.

By the time they reached the door, they were damp. They were also laughing as they stepped inside.

"Promise me you won't look backward anymore," Leah said before withdrawing her arm from Rebecca's. "I want us to be friends."

Rebecca gave her a tentative look. "Could we perhaps be sisters?"

"Yes, please." Leah moved toward her then stopped abruptly, her gaze uncertain. "May I hug you?"

The question froze Rebecca cold. She'd been hugged a few times by Aunt Jennet since Horatio's death, but never by anyone else. "I don't—" Struggling to find words, she said, "We never did that."

"No. It is not how we were raised. However, Phin

has always been very keen about hugging, as is his family." Leah paused before adding, "I'll understand if you'd rather not, but if you decide you'd like to try it, I'm always game."

Rebecca thought back to when she was first married, about how she'd been looking forward to the touching part of marriage—not the sex, but the affectionate touches one saw some married couples engage in. Not Rebecca's parents, however. But living in Marrywell, one saw plenty of demonstrative examples of people who loved and cared for one another.

"I would like a hug," Rebecca admitted.

Leah smiled before enveloping Rebecca in a tight embrace.

Closing her eyes, Rebecca almost couldn't accept what was happening. She'd hoped for forgiveness and perhaps had dreamed of reconciliation. It seemed she might have the family she wanted, or at least a sister. Who also came with a brother-in-law and, soon, a niece or nephew.

Warmth spread through Rebecca as she thought of having a child in her life. He or she would not be hers, but they would be the next best thing: family.

Suddenly, she wanted to see if she could expand this, to reclaim her other siblings and perhaps even their father. That seemed overwhelming at the moment, and she decided she should take one thing at a time.

Rebecca realized they were standing at the edge of the ballroom. Perhaps they were drawing attention. This would look...odd. "Should we stop?" she whispered.

"I suppose I should return to my duties," Leah said with a sigh.

They parted and giggled at the same time.

"I can't believe you're the May Queen," Rebecca said. "Were you a maiden fair last year?"

"Goodness, no. I was companion to a young lady from London, and she was a maiden fair. I'll tell you all about it some time." Leah looked about the ballroom. "Where is your employer?"

"I don't know, but I should find him. I hope he won't mind that I was gone so long." Rebecca would apologize. When he'd encouraged her to take a respite, he surely hadn't meant for her to disappear.

Leah laughed softly. "I highly doubt that since he's the one who told me where to find you."

He had? How unexpected. Or was it? He'd been incredibly supportive of her last night and seemed to want to help her set things right with Leah.

"There he is," Leah said. "You can barely see him amidst that gaggle of young women."

Rebecca followed her sister's nod across the room and indeed could just make out his dark head with its extreme, overpomaded hairstyle. "I must go rescue him."

"He doesn't like the attention?" Leah asked. "I'm afraid he's doomed since he's a marquess at a matchmaking festival with a matchmaker. He is easily the most eligible man here—a nobleman who is looking to wed."

"Except he has...requirements. I doubt most of those young women will meet them." Rebecca was anxious to help him. "Please excuse me. I must see to him."

"Of course. Do let me know if I can help. I am the May Queen, after all." Leah winked at her.

Rebecca quickly took herself off. Creslow was in desperate need of assistance.

CHAPTER 7

*T*he swarm of young ladies was trying even Nash's patience. He could typically charm and flirt all night long. Doing so, in fact, was what he was known for. But this unfettered and unabashed attention by so many directed completely at him was unlike anything he'd ever experienced.

Apparently, it didn't matter that he'd tried to make himself less attractive. He hadn't helped himself by being gregarious at first, but now he stood with his arms crossed in an attempt to keep the masses away. It still wasn't enough. He set his lips into a deep frown.

"What's wrong, my lord?" asked a fresh-faced young lady with round brown eyes.

Before he could grunt in response, Mrs. Sweet arrived outside the press. Their gazes met, and he sent her a silent plea. She threaded her way through the young ladies, tilting her head this way and that as she murmured things he couldn't hear. He could only see her lips move. And what lovely lips they were.

When at last she reached him, she gave the young ladies a bright smile. "Forgive us, but Lord Creslow is due to speak with someone." She clutched his arm and guided him through the throng.

"Thank you," he whispered. "I was growing most desperate."

She steered him out of the ballroom and into an antechamber where refreshments were laid out on tables. "I could see that."

"There were just so many of them. I'm slightly embarrassed. Typically, I can hold my own. However, I've never been beset like *that*. I'm used to some decorum in London."

"You are *not* in London, as you've learned. They meant no harm. Did you feel threatened?"

"I did not. As you predicted, it was overwhelming. They were asking how I'm enjoying Marrywell, if I would be at the ball, and whether I would dance. One young lady boldly asked if I would partner her."

Her brow creased. "You weren't upset by any of that, were you?"

"Not at all. I just didn't know what to *do*." He lifted his hands in defeat. "My usual charm utterly failed me."

She smiled. "I find that hard to believe, but I don't doubt you. I apologize for abandoning you for so long. I shan't do it again."

"I didn't mind. You were taking care of important business, I hope."

"Have you always been a meddler?" she asked drily.

"Not at all." He grimaced. "Are you annoyed with me?"

"No," she said softly, her gaze warming. "I would have told you not to do it, but I'm glad you did."

"It went well, then?"

"Better than I ever imagined. Thank you." She adopted a more businesslike demeanor. "I daresay you seem to be doing a fine job of executing the plan to meet as many potential brides as possible. Let us attempt to find some that are of a more...mature nature. If that's acceptable to you?"

"Let me have a cake and a glass of sherry, and nearly anything will be acceptable to me."

After he indulged himself, they returned to the ballroom. Mrs. Sweet curated whom they spoke with, steering him in one direction to meet a woman in her later twenties and then another to meet a few others who were more reserved than those who'd clamored after him earlier.

As they moved away from one of them, Mrs. Sweet leaned close and asked, "Have you met any ladies today who might satisfy your requirements?"

"How can I?" he responded in an equally low tone. "We didn't present my arrangement to any of them."

"I mean the physical attraction aspect. Do any of them...stir you to *want* to discuss your arrangement?"

Not a one. But he hesitated to say so. Mrs. Sweet was working awfully hard, and it wasn't her fault that the only woman he'd encountered that day who *stirred* him was her.

She frowned at him. "I can see the answer is no. Shall we continue, or would you rather wave a white flag and return to the inn?"

He sensed a frustration simmering beneath the outwardly pleasant demeanor she'd possessed all afternoon as she sought to find him a wife. "Let us return to the inn. I think we will both benefit from a respite before tonight's ball."

They retrieved their hats and departed. It wasn't raining any longer, so they walked back along the High Street toward the Buck and Maiden. Her frown seemed to deepen, and her forehead creased into more furrows as they progressed.

"Are you upset?" he asked.

"I'd hoped things would go better today, that a woman or two would pique your interest." She flicked him an apologetic glance. "I'm sorry there aren't more mature ladies from your social class."

"My bride doesn't need to come from a titled family."

"She should at least be from your class. She oughtn't be—" She hesitated a moment before finishing, "Like me."

They'd turned onto the street where the Buck and Maiden was located.

"I would have no quarrel with a bride who is like you," he said, admiring her profile with its pert nose and full lips.

She turned her head. "You'd marry a farmer's daughter?"

"Why not? If we shared common interests and a mutual attraction, I should feel fortunate."

"I can't imagine that's true. What if she doesn't know the first thing about fashion? Or can't comport herself well with your important friends and associates? Or isn't aware of the difference between a duke and a knight?"

"Titles are bloody confusing," he said. "Don't fret. The festival has barely started. I'm sure we'll find someone who fits what I'm looking for."

"I'm afraid I don't share your confidence. I'm concerned you're going to be fighting off gaggles of young ladies who don't interest you all week." She paused as they walked up the path to the inn. "I must confess I am beginning to doubt how I may help you."

"How did you make your other matches?"

"I noted common interests between the two parties, and a mutual…affinity. Or curiosity." She looked upward as she gently shook her head. "I don't know. I just sensed there was something connecting them." She lowered her gaze to his, and he saw something that enchanted him: wonder.

"What was that?" he asked, feeling slightly breathless.

"Love, I suppose?" She lifted a shoulder. "I can't be sure as I have little to no experience with that emotion."

She'd never been in love. An ache spread through him, but it wasn't the familiar pain of lost love. No, it was the thought of never having experienced it at all. He sometimes thought that would have been better, but in this moment, he knew he would not have traded his love with Louisa for anything, even knowing he would lose her.

"But you're clearly able to recognize it in others," he said softly. Perhaps she wasn't going to be able to help him after all. She saw love as it bloomed, and he refused to allow that to happen.

"The clouds are darkening again," she said, interrupting his thoughts. "We should go in."

Nash moved to open the door for her, and they walked inside. After exchanging pleasantries with the innkeeper, they went upstairs. He stopped outside her room. "What time should we leave tonight?"

"Eight. I'll be dining in my room, in case you were planning to eat together. I don't have time to dine downstairs."

"Understandable," he said, though he would miss her company.

"Let's see how the ball goes tonight. Perhaps you just haven't encountered the right woman yet. I will keep a close eye on you and the ladies with whom you interact. I am hopeful I will detect a mutual interest that could progress into what you are looking for. It's just going to take time. Thankfully, we have a week." She gave him an encouraging smile.

A week in which to find a woman whose company he would enjoy enough to marry, but not to love. He was beginning to think his requirements would be impossible to meet.

"If anyone can do it, you will." He turned to go, but she briefly touched his sleeve, drawing him to pivot back toward her.

"Thank you again for sending Leah outside." She cocked her head. "Why did you do it?"

"I hoped you would feel better. Do you?" He held his breath.

She smiled, and there was a not insignificant fluttering in his chest. "Yes."

He exhaled. "Good."

He watched her go into her room before turning toward his. When he was closed inside, he tossed his hat onto a chair and stripped his coat away, laying it over the back of the same chair.

What was he doing at this matchmaking festival? Did he really think he would find a woman who would be content as his marchioness? He wasn't sure that woman existed.

Why not *here?* a voice in the back of his mind responded. *You just need to meet and get to know someone, to determine if they might be amenable to your arrangement.*

Except the only woman he'd met and wanted to know better was his matchmaker. His gaze moved to the door that led to Mrs. Sweet's room.

Groaning, he turned away and went into his bedchamber. This was a hopeless endeavor. He needed a marchioness, but he didn't really want one. Actually, what he needed was an heir. That was the primary duty, wasn't it? Ensure the family line? To what end? Did any of that really matter?

He wiped his hand over his face. These were the questions that had plagued him after Louisa's death. Loving her and losing her so soon made everything seem so pointless. Why love anyone when it couldn't last?

Only it did last. And that was the pain of it. To love someone and not be able to be with them, to talk to them, to hold them… There was no greater anguish.

Nash went to the bottle of port that he'd requested the night before and poured a glass. He drank half of it, welcoming the sweet balm. It had been a frequent friend in the days and months following Louisa's death, and never failed to remind him of her.

But now it also made him think of his matchmaker and the night they'd met. That had been before he'd known her name. Rebecca Sweet.

Rebecca.

He wished he could call her that, for that would mean they were more familiar. More intimate. Which they had been. Once.

Taking another drink, he tried to banish both women from his mind. However, Mrs. Sweet—Rebecca—remained. She was right next door. He could still taste the velvet of her tongue and the silk of her sex. His cock hardened.

This was becoming an obsession.

Was it because they hadn't finished their night together? If they did that, could he forget about her? He couldn't say.

Lifting the glass toward his mouth, he froze. Would Rebecca accept his arrangement? They shared a physical attraction. Or they had, anyway.

Did she even wish to marry again? She'd launched a matchmaking career, so perhaps independence was her true desire.

Even so, he could offer her that—or a version of it —as his marchioness. She would have whatever she wanted. All he asked in return was her loyalty. Nash had witnessed how his father's philandering had worn on his mother, how withdrawn she'd become before his death six years earlier.

Since then, she'd come into the light again and found a renaissance. She'd taken up residence in Bath, cultivated a group of friends who shared her love of art and literature, and hosted regular salons. She was, in a word, thriving, and Nash could not have been happier. She was proof that romantic love was not necessary to find joy and fulfillment.

He doubted loyalty would be a problem for Rebecca, as it sounded as though her former husband had been unfaithful. Perhaps she would be open to becoming his marchioness. It seemed a reasonable solution. *If* she wanted to remarry.

Given her experience, she might not. Particularly if her matchmaking career seemed destined for success. He wanted that for her—success and satisfaction however she wanted it. She deserved that and hoped she realized that too. He smiled, glad that the meeting between her and her sister in the garden had gone well. He'd risked Rebecca's anger, sticking his nose into her business, but he'd thought it was worth the hazard.

He finished his port and went to the dressing room to ring for Martin.

Yes, he'd find out if Rebecca was open to remarriage. And if she was, he could forget all about this matchmaking business. Best of all, he could have Rebecca in his arms again. Mayhap even tonight.

❧

*R*ebecca had received a note from her sister that the crowning ceremony and welcome ball would be held at the assembly rooms due to the rain. Pity, for there was nothing so magical as the

botanical gardens alight with lanterns and the palpable anticipation for the revelation of the maidens
fair.

Years ago, at her first festival as a marriageable
young lady, Rebecca had prayed to be chosen, for it
would have made her mother exceedingly happy.
Maidens fair typically had no difficulty receiving a
proposal by the end of the festival. Though Rebecca
had not been a maiden fair, she had found a match.

As Rebecca descended the stairs and entered the
common room, Creslow was already waiting for her.
His gaze moved over her with an appreciative precision that made her body quiver. She took a deep
breath to try to calm her racing pulse.

Unlike that afternoon when he'd attempted to
look less attractive, tonight, he was dressed impec-
cably in black with an artfully knotted snow-white
cravat. His hair was immaculately styled with just the
right amount of pomade. Or perhaps there was none
at all. The dark locks looked thick and lush, and she
wanted to run her hands through the sable thatch.

Damn, she'd been doing such a fine job of ignoring his finer attributes.

"You look stunning this evening, Mrs. Sweet. That
green is a splendid color with your hair and eyes. Indeed, it almost makes your eyes appear the same
color as the ocean."

"You are too kind. Thank you." She bit the inside
of her lip lest she prattle on about how glorious he
looked. "Are you aware the evening's activities will
now be held in the assembly rooms?"

"I am. Given the poor weather, I thought it best
we take my coach."

"Is your rule in effect, about whatever happens in
the carriage staying in the carriage?"

He smiled. "Always."

"Have you used that phrase to flirt with many women?"

When he laughed, his dark eyes glittered. "Not until you."

A silly burst of joy spread through her.

"Ready?" he asked.

"Yes."

A footman stood at the door and opened it. Then he held an umbrella over Rebecca as she hurried to the coach. Creslow helped her inside and climbed in after her. They were quickly on their way. The journey would only take about five minutes, perhaps a little longer if there was a long line. At least they would be dry.

They sat together on the same seat again, and Rebecca was eager to focus on something other than his proximity. Because it was chilly, she found she wanted to press against him for warmth. Yes, definitely just for his body heat.

She glanced at him, careful not to lean toward him. "I was thinking we should perhaps search for any widows in attendance. We might have more luck with them."

He cast her a sideways look, his mouth twisting into a faint grimace. "A widow interested in remarrying... Would you consider it?"

Was he asking her specifically? As in, would she consider wedding him? No, of course not. He was merely posing the question to her as a widow. "I'm not certain I would. I'm enjoying my independence. It would have to be for the right reason, and I'd need to be sure."

"What reason is that?"

"Unlike you, I would *only* remarry for love." She realized that was the only way she'd be willing to cede her independence.

His gaze slid away from hers. "I can see why that would be important to you."

"And I see that not marrying for love is important to you, even if I don't entirely understand it."

"Did you think you were in love when you wed before?" He looked toward her once more.

"I thought I could be. I was smitten. But I was also looking for a way out of Marrywell, as you astutely discerned. Horatio was attentive and kind during our courtship. I was eager for a family of my own, and he shared my desire for children. I had every expectation we would find happiness together."

"But there were no children, and the Horatio of your courtship was not the Horatio of your marriage."

"Exactly so." She hadn't thought she would leave her depressing childhood home and end up in an equally miserable situation. "I was lonely."

He took her hand again, as he had the other night. "I hate thinking that. You should have joy every single day. What makes you happy, Mrs. Sweet?"

She took a moment to answer as the coach came to a stop. "I'm not sure I know." She looked over at him. "What makes *you* happy?"

"Sitting in carriages with a lovely woman sharing confidences." He gave her an almost wicked smile. "I also enjoy attending the theatre, visiting museums, studying architecture, and reading books, which you already know, of course. Do you like any of those things?"

"I've never been to the theatre. Or a museum. And you know I like books."

"What about companionship?" he asked. "Would that make you happy?"

"What sort of companionship?" The air in the coach had shifted. Thickened, if that were even possible. Her breathing became a bit shallow.

"Male companionship. Not all men are like your husband. I suggested you consider taking a lover."

"I wouldn't know how to do that," she said, feeling warm. The coach inched along at an interminable pace. She glanced out the window to verify that they were in a queue to the assembly rooms. "And I don't want you to offer your help again."

"What if I offered me instead?"

She snapped her head toward him and clenched her jaw to keep from gaping. "You can't do that, not while you're looking for a wife."

"That's true, but I've been thinking I should postpone that endeavor."

He no longer wanted to find a match at the festival? "Are you serious?"

He inclined his head. "I may be, as it seems rather challenging in this environment."

"We could leave the festival," she offered, though she wasn't sure where they would go.

"No, it's not just that." He hesitated before continuing, his eyes fixed on hers. "It's you. I like you. I'm attracted to you. I feel as though we have unfinished business."

Yes, that *exactly*.

Rebecca could feel her heart beating in her ears. "It must remain that way. Do you approve of my plan to search for widows?"

He blinked, his eyes shuttering. Then he turned his head away from her entirely. Whatever connection they'd shared a moment earlier was gone. "It sounds more than reasonable."

A footman from the assembly rooms opened the door to the coach, and the marquess stepped down. As she put her hand in his and descended to the pavement, she tried not to think of what might have been. If she'd met Creslow years ago—before he'd met and lost his wife and vowed never to love again.

If they'd finished their night together at the house party.

She couldn't be his wife, and she shouldn't be his lover. And she was starting to think she oughtn't be his matchmaker either.

CHAPTER 8

The crowning ceremony was surprisingly heartwarming, but Nash attributed that to watching Rebecca see her sister crowned as the May Queen. She'd dashed the tears away before they'd fallen, but Nash had seen them. Whatever happened with his bride hunt, he would always be glad his matchmaker had found her way home.

The first dance was traditionally led by the May King and Queen along with the new maidens fair and their partners, whom they selected. That meant that Nash had danced the first dance because one of the maidens fair had come straight for him. In truth, two others had looked as though they also meant to ask him, but hadn't been fast enough.

Following that dance, Nash had hidden himself away behind a potted plant. There, he'd been treated to a rather amorous display as the Earl of Gilbourne had locked lips with an attractive young lady. Since the earl was typically never without a giant stick up his arse, Nash was glad to see him loosening up.

Nash was not glad to hear that Rebecca would only remarry for love. So much for his new and improved marchioness plan.

Dammit, he was brooding. And that would apparently only draw the ladies to him. He needed to summon a more cheerful attitude. Not *too* cheerful, however, lest that also encourage the young ladies. Bloody hell, this was difficult. Perhaps he ought to just call it a night and return to the Buck and Maiden. He would send the coach back for Rebecca.

"You look a bit glum this evening, Nash."

Turning, Nash saw Phin, whom he hadn't heard approach. "Evening, Phin." The man had insisted he call him that, and so Nash had also insisted he employ the same familiarity.

Phin inclined his head. "I'm not generally one to give advice, especially on matters of the heart, but I don't think you'll attract a bride with that dark brow you're sporting."

Matters of the heart had nothing to do with Nash's search for a wife, but he wasn't going to point that out. "I'm not entirely sure I want one," Nash said. "A bride, that is."

"Do you feel as if you need one?" Phin asked. "Since you're a marquess, I imagine you've a sense of duty about that."

"I do, but I'm not convinced marriage is for me."

"Ah, yes. I understand you were married before. I'm sorry for your loss."

The pain felt different tonight. Not as acute. "Thank you."

"I've found marriage to be wonderful." Phin practically beamed. His happiness was like a tangible thing, a bright cloak he wore around himself for all the world to see and admire. And perhaps envy.

"That's splendid." Nash didn't say what else he was thinking, that he prayed Phin and Leah never experienced the heartache he had.

"I'm sure you'll discover what's best for you," Phin said. "The matchmaking festival is strangely accurate, even when one isn't on the hunt."

"You weren't looking to wed?" Nash asked.

"On the contrary, I was hoping to land an heiress." He grimaced. "My father made some poor investment choices, and the gardens are a great expense. However, I fell in love with Leah. As it happened, she was an heiress, but we didn't know that at the time. And two years ago, our friend Sadie ended up hosting a duke whose coach lost a wheel in front of their farm. The last thing she expected was to fall in love and become a duchess, but that's precisely what happened."

"Ah, Lawford. Yes, I've met his duchess in London. She's delightful." Nash hadn't remembered that they met at the matchmaking festival.

"They're here somewhere, if you'd care to see them," Phin said.

While Nash would have liked that, he preferred his idea of returning to the Buck and Maiden. "I'll look for them tomorrow. I've a headache, which is why I likely appear glum." He gave Phin a quick smile. "I think I must return to the inn. Would you let Mrs. Sweet know that I've gone? I'll send the coach back for her. She need only ask a page for it when she's ready to depart."

Phin's brow creased. "Shouldn't you tell her yourself? She may wish to leave with you."

"I don't want to interrupt her evening. She looks to be having a wonderful time. It pleases me to see her and your wife enjoying their time together."

"It does me too," Phin agreed with a nod. "Leah told me what you did earlier today. I can't thank you enough. She is so glad to have her sister."

"Families should be together." Because when they were torn apart by death, that was no longer possible. "Good night, Phin."

"Night, Nash."

As Nash made his way to the entry hall, he pondered his matchmaking conundrum. He really had lost all taste for it, at least for now. He was rather obsessed with Rebecca. With seeing her happy, with finishing whatever had sparked between them at his cousin's house party.

A page appeared, and Nash gave the lad a shilling to fetch his coach.

"We aren't supposed to take money, my lord," the boy, who was probably around twelve, said.

"I won't tell if you won't." Nash winked at him. The page grinned as he hurried off.

By the time Nash was settled in the coach, he'd conceived a possible resolution. There was really nothing else he could do. There was nothing else he *wanted* to do.

The question was what Rebecca wanted. And he hoped to find out.

~

*R*ebecca spent more than an hour searching for widows and observing ladies to see if they might suit the marquess. She was finding this task more and more unappealing. Was that because she felt uneasy about matching people without the presence of love, or was it because she couldn't stop thinking of how Creslow had told her that he was attracted to her, that they had "unfinished business"?

It was both, she realized. For every young lady she watched, she noted a couple who seemed to be in the throes of flirtation or mutual attraction. Eyes fluttering and fixing on one another, fleeting touches, secret smiles. It was heartwarming to watch and at the same time depressing as Rebecca reminded herself that she wasn't looking for such connection—for the marquess. For herself, she would be thrilled to experience that. For real this time.

Did she want to find her own match? To fall in love and remarry instead of continuing as a matchmaker? It was an intriguing thought, but then she recalled that her efforts at love, both romantic and otherwise, had utterly failed. She was better off keeping her eye on the plan she'd executed: find success as a matchmaker and rely only on herself.

Phin approached her with an intent expression. "Ah, there you are, Rebecca."

"Evening, Phin. I see Leah is quite busy. I hope she doesn't get too tired."

"I plan to rescue her momentarily and insist upon a short respite." He gave her a warm smile. "It's wonderful to see you caring for her." A look of horror tripped across his features. "I didn't mean to imply that you didn't. It's just...well, you're here. And you've reconciled. And I'm so pleased." He shook his head. "My apologies."

Rebecca touched his arm. "There's no need for you to apologize. I know what you mean. It is wonderful, and I'm incredibly grateful to have Leah in my life once more. I *do* care for her, and I will ensure she never doubts that."

"I don't think she ever did," Phin said softly. "But she's so happy to have you here. I do hope you'll stay longer than the festival. She'd love to have you at Radford Grange. As would I. Our door is always open to you."

"I've been considering staying. I appreciate your kind invitation. Now, go and rescue my poor sister."

"In a moment. I actually came over to tell you that Nash has returned to the inn with a headache. He's sent the coach back for you for whenever you wish to leave."

He'd left without seeing her himself? Rebecca couldn't help feeling disappointed.

"I see. Thank you for telling me. Please give my

best to Leah. I'm going to return to the inn." There was no point in staying if the marquess had left.

A short while later, she entered the inn and walked up to her room. She looked down the corridor toward Creslow's door. Was he already asleep? It was early yet.

The urge to knock on his door and ask why he hadn't told her himself that he was leaving was strong, but if he wasn't feeling well, she couldn't blame him. Perhaps it was that she wanted to tend to him, to help him the way he'd helped her with Leah.

Instead, she went into her room and removed her cloak and gloves. Then she kicked off her shoes. Eager to be rid of her evening finery and to loosen her hair from the abundance of pins the inn's lady's maid had employed, Rebecca went to her dressing room. When she emerged a short while later, she felt infinitely more comfortable with her hair plaited to the side, and garbed in her nightclothes, including a thick dressing gown to guard against the chill. So far, this festival's weather had been disappointing. Hopefully, things would improve.

There was a full day of activities tomorrow, and she and the marquess hadn't decided what they would do. Perhaps it was best if they didn't focus so much on finding a bride. At least for tomorrow. Rebecca would continue to hope the perfect match was out there, that they simply hadn't met her yet.

She glanced at the door that led to Creslow's room. Should she knock on it and discuss her plan for tomorrow with him? No, she wouldn't be that forward, nor did she wish to disturb him. She'd write a note and have a footman deliver it.

Going to the writing desk, she noticed a piece of parchment—a letter—and a bank note. Brow furrowing, she picked up the bank note first. It was written by the marquess for the amount of her fee. Keeping it in her hand, she lifted the letter and read the contents. Her eyes widened with each line.

He was terminating her employment? Effective *immediately*? She read it again.

*W*hile I appreciate your services, I have decided this is neither the time nor place for me to find a bride. This is not a reflection on you or your abilities. You have gone above and beyond to try to meet my unique requirements. I am grateful for your time and effort.

*B*uried beneath her irritation that he'd informed her of this decision in writing instead of in person was a subtle but welcome relief. Now she wouldn't have to find a woman who would accept a marriage without love.

Forward or not and without concern for his aching head, if he even had one, she stalked to the adjoining door. Transferring the letter to the hand with the bank note, she banged the heel of her now-free hand on the wood. She continued the racket until the door rattled.

"I can't open it," he said from the other side. "You'll need to unlock your side."

Throwing the bolt, she pushed open the door. He stood in his banyan—the very same green velvet garment he'd worn at that bloody house party. Why did it have to be *that* one?

She waved the letter and bank note in his face. "What is this?"

"I should think it was clear." He sounded confused. Good, so was she.

"First, you abandon me at the ball, and now you terminate my employment with a letter?" She stared at him, her pulse galloping. "Have I offended you somehow?"

"Heavens, no! I didn't wish to intrude on your festive evening. As for the letter, that is typically what one does when conducting business."

She narrowed her eyes at him. "Oh, *now* we're just business associates, after all your friendship prattle."

He grimaced. "I wasn't going to leave without seeing you or anything."

"What a relief. And what am I to do now that I've been dismissed by a marquess? The least you could have done is offer to write me a letter of recommendation."

"Yes, yes, of course. I would be happy to do that. Thrilled. Ecstatic. I'll write as many as you like to whomever you like." He looked at her with concern. "I'll do whatever I can to help you secure your next client. This is my failure, not yours."

Her pulse began to slow, and she lowered her arm so that she clutched the bank note and letter at her side. "What are you going to do about marrying?"

He shrugged, and she realized he was holding a glass of what looked to be port. "I must do so at some point, but it doesn't need to be here or now. I confess the festival, or rather its attendees, have overwhelmed me."

"Is that the only reason you've changed your mind?" As soon as she asked the question, she wished she hadn't. It wasn't her business.

There was a long, heavy silence before he answered. Her pulse sped again, and she was all too aware that they were in his bedchamber—or at least his sitting room—in their nightclothes. And there was no footman who would interrupt them, nor any risk of being caught alone together.

"No," he said, his voice deep and thick. "That is not the only reason." He set his glass down on a small table and came toward her, his gait slow and measured. "I am finding it altogether impossible to determine if any of the women at this festival might interest me because all my focus, indeed to the point of near obsession, is directed entirely on *you*."

Rebecca swallowed. His words were as arousing as any caress. No one had ever spoken to her in such a way.

"I had to leave the ball because once I concluded that the only thing I wanted was to have an affair with you, I realized you could no longer be in my employ."

Her body heated with desire. "You didn't have a headache?"

"No."

Rebecca let that answer sink into her, along with his seductive gaze. "If I declined to engage in an...affair, would you rehire me as your matchmaker?"

"No. I don't want to find a match. At least not right now. I don't know that I can while this connection between us exists. I would finish what we started at that house party. But if you don't share my longing, tell me, and I won't bother you again."

Temptation bent her toward him. She absolutely shared his longing; however, she didn't know if she wanted an affair. What would that even entail?

It seemed she had two choices. She could refuse him and return to her room, perhaps never to see him again. Or she could surrender to temptation. An affair wasn't necessary. All they needed was one night—the night they would have spent together.

Rebecca took a deep breath and spoke deliberately. "I would like to finish that night. One night." She watched as his nostrils flared and his eyes glittered. "Tonight."

He closed the space between them, but didn't yet touch her. "Tonight." Lifting his hand to her face, he gently stroked her cheek with his knuckles. "Rebecca. Can you imagine how many nights I dreamed of you, and I'd no name to put to your beautiful face?"

"You dreamed of me?"

"Countless times." He tucked a lock of her hair behind her ear and caressed her before tugging gently on her lobe. "Did you not think of me too?"

"How could I not? You gave me something I'd never had. And if you had regret, well, I had staggering disappointment."

He laughed, then sobered quickly. "I shouldn't find amusement in that."

"It's all right. I said it with humor. I've been working to let my bitterness go. It isn't always easy, but meeting you helped," she added softly.

His lips curled in a heart-stopping smile. "Then allow me to help even more, if I may."

Anticipation stole Rebecca's breath. She dropped the papers she held to the floor and clasped the front of his dressing gown. "You may. Now."

Angling his head, he kissed her. Their lips met, and she was instantly cast into a decadent bliss. There was nothing gentle or tentative, just a fiery joining that tore through her with an incomparable need.

Rebecca pressed against him and twined her arms around his neck as he clasped her waist. One of his hands moved up her spine while the other cupped her backside, bringing her hips flush to his. She felt the length of him and rotated her pelvis, desperate for his touch any way she could get it.

They kissed and kissed again, exploring each other with lips and tongues, as their hands made their own discoveries upon each other's bodies. He unfastened her dressing gown and pushed it from her shoulders. She shrugged the garment away, letting it drop to the floor. Then she performed the same task for him.

Except when his dressing gown fell away, she was met with the warmth of his bare flesh. She looked down at his body and found it utterly naked. Her gaze fixed on the hard length of his cock. "You don't wear a nightshirt?"

He grinned. "Not unless it's terribly cold. I find I've been nearly always overheated since becoming reacquainted with you the other day."

"It's just...I've never seen a man without a stitch of clothing. Mind you, I'm not sure I would have wanted to see my husband in that fashion." She shuddered.

"He wore clothing when he came to your bed?"

"He made sure it was dark."

"I have no such plan." He swung her into his arms.

She gasped. "What are you doing?"

"Carrying you to my bed, where I will lay you down. Then I plan to light more candles."

Rebecca giggled. As he took her over the threshold into his bedchamber, she found there was enough light for her to see him. "You don't have to. I think I'll be able to study you quite well."

He set her on the bed and arched a brow. "Study me? Shall I administer a test later?"

"I've no idea what that would entail, but I'll leave that to you." She knelt on the bed and raked her gaze over his form. He stood there, tall and erect—his shoulders, his spine, and his cock.

The muscles of his chest and abdomen were as sculpted as the lines of his face, prompting her to ask if he came from clay. Or perhaps marble.

Laughing, he said no. "I do box a couple of times a week."

"I should like to watch that." She reached her hand out to touch him, then paused.

"Go ahead," he urged. "Please."

She placed her palm against him. "You are rather warm," she murmured. "And so exquisite."

Putting her other hand on him, she skimmed her hands over his chest and shoulders, then down his abdomen, where a dark trail of hair led to his sex. "Is it...permissible to touch you there?"

"Of course." He said it as if she ought to have known.

She blushed. "I didn't know. There will be much I don't know, I'm afraid."

"I'm an ass," he whispered before kissing her. He clasped the back of her head, holding her while he tasted her with languorous, deliberate strokes of his tongue. When he pulled back, she was breathless. He looked into her eyes. "Ask me anything. Ask *for* anything. This night is for you."

She fixed on the dark chocolate brown of his irises. "This night is for *us*. You were the one who was left *completely* wanting last time." She put her fingertips on the tip of his sex. "What shall I do?"

He sucked in a breath and half smiled. "Wrap your hand around me and slide it from base to tip."

"Like the act when you're inside." She knew that much, at least.

"Exactly."

She began to stroke him, just as he said. He closed his eyes, and his head fell back, his lips parted. Smiling to herself, Rebecca leaned forward and kissed the hollow at the base of his neck. He still held her head, and now his fingers dug gently into her scalp.

Encouraged, she licked his flesh before kissing along his collarbone. She continued to move her hand along his length while she explored his chest with her mouth. His breathing became shallow, and he let out a soft moan.

"Rebecca." He murmured her name as his hips began to move. "Faster. Please."

Her own sex was heavy and wet with need. This was an arousal akin to the first time she'd met him. How could she be so ready for him when he'd barely touched her? That had never happened with Horatio.

Because her body knew the marquess, even from that one encounter.

She could not keep calling him the marquess. "Nash," she tried.

His head came up, and his eyes opened. "Yes?"

"I think I want you to touch me."

"As I said, I am yours to command." He grasped the hem of her night rail and pulled the garment over her head, which meant she had to release his cock. "Lie back on the bed. Spread your legs and show me how much you want me to touch you."

His words stoked her already desperate desire. She reclined on the bed and did as he said, though it felt strange to expose herself in such a manner.

"So beautiful." He climbed onto the bed and positioned himself between her legs on his knees. "Your nipples are already puckered." Slowly falling forward, he licked one of her breasts before closing his mouth over her and sucking.

She gripped his head as sensation streaked through her. Her sex pulsed, and her hips arched off the bed.

He seemed to know exactly what she needed, for he skimmed his hand along her inner thigh and stroked along the folds of her sex before finding that nub that had apparently not existed until that night in the library at Clipstone Hedge. He pressed and worked her hungry flesh until she writhed.

"Please. Nash. I need you."

"How do you need me, love?" He drew on her

nipple before kissing between her breasts and
moving to the other one.

"Inside me. I want to feel you. I want to...come
with you inside me. I've never done that."

"Then I shall be honored if you will with me." He
slid his finger into her sheath. "You are plenty wet.
Bring your legs up now, bend your knees."

She did, though her thighs were quivering. He
moved closer, and his hand left her sex. She whimpered, aching from the loss, but he soon returned.
The tip of his cock pressed against her. Then he
thrust inside, moving slowly.

Her hips rose to meet him, and she grasped at his
back and waist, eager to be fully joined. He leaned
down to kiss her, his body covering hers as he seated
himself within her.

She returned his kiss and wrapped her legs
around his waist. He began to move, slowly at first,
but always driving deep into her. She felt as though
she were being stretched taut, her body desperate for
release. Then he went faster, stroking in and out, increasing the friction so she moaned and whimpered.

Clasping him more tightly with her legs, she
gripped his back and moved her body with his. *Yes,
faster, harder.*

He kissed her temple. "Whatever you desire."

Had she spoken out loud? She must have, for he
increased his speed until he was driving into her with
hard, swift thrusts. Her body began to quiver, her
muscles tightening. Overwhelming pleasure
slammed against her and lifted her. She went completely rigid.

Then she fell to pieces.

He moved even faster, and somehow, her pleasure
increased. She clung to him as a torrent of ecstasy
threatened to carry her away. Suddenly, he was gone.

While this was another new experience, she knew why he was doing it—to prevent a child.

He fell to the side of her as her body began to calm. A deep satisfaction settled into her bones. But there was a tinge of sadness. Because of what he'd done. Or hadn't done, really.

Since she'd never conceived with Horatio, there was a chance she couldn't. But as he'd never fathered a child with any of his mistresses, she'd held out hope that she could be a mother.

To do that, however, she needed to be a wife, and she wasn't going to marry Nash. Was that the real reason for her sadness?

CHAPTER 9

*N*ash briefly left the bed to tidy himself. When he returned, Rebecca had snuggled under the bedclothes. He slipped in to join her.

She lay on her back, her gaze fixed on the ceiling. Her expression did not reflect the level of bliss that he might have expected, given how much she'd seemed to enjoy herself.

"All right?" he asked, moving to her side and facing her.

"Oh, yes." She flashed him a smile. "I think I'm perhaps overwhelmed. That was a unique experience."

"Does that mean you enjoyed it?"

She turned toward him. "Very much. Are you planning to leave tomorrow?"

"I don't have to. What are your plans?"

"I'd arranged for transportation back to Leighton Buzzard at the end of the festival, but I may stay longer to visit with Leah."

"I hope you do." He couldn't stop staring at her. Much of her red hair had come loose from its plait. The color was so vibrant and beautiful. At this distance, he could see all the faint freckles that tracked across her upper cheeks and nose. They were so unique and charming, but then so was she.

She was a woman with an indomitable spirit, someone who'd fought for a better life for herself, for happiness. And so far, she'd been rather unfortunate in that regard. He hoped she was now on a better path, and he was glad to be a small part of it.

"Are you asking for more than tonight?" she asked.

"I would certainly be amenable to that. But if I stay in Marrywell, it's entirely because of you. I don't want to participate in the matchmaking aspect of the festival." Whatever happened this week with Rebecca, he wanted to focus completely on her, on the limited time they might share. "Does that interest you? We only discussed one night, but I'm not sure it's enough. For me," he added, hoping she felt the same.

"I wouldn't mind continuing," she said, perhaps a little shyly. "We'll make it known that you've decided not to wed." Her mouth ticked up in a half smile. "Or, we can just spend all our time in the brewer's field, which is perhaps the only place where you won't be besieged by marriage-minded ladies and their mothers."

Nash laughed. "You've convinced me that the brewer's field is my salvation. Though, I would prefer we don't spend *all* our time there." He scooted closer to her and slipped his arm around her waist.

"I'd like to visit Black Sheep Farm tomorrow." She snagged her lower lip with her teeth, and while she likely had no idea how seductive she looked doing that, Nash's body was well aware. "That's where I grew up. My father and brother—and his family— still live there."

"Would you like company? We can take my coach —if it's far enough to require a coach. I'll even wait inside it if you'd prefer to visit them alone."

"I'm not sure I want to explain why my client is visiting my family with me," she said. "That seems odd. So yes, it may be best if you wait in the carriage. Unless..." She narrowed her eyes at him. "Are you just trying to lure me into the coach?"

He laughed, then kissed her cheek. "No, but that's not a bad idea." He trailed kisses toward her ear and then down her neck. "However, I'm not sure that's necessary when this bed seems to be working perfectly well."

She clutched his head as he licked and suckled at the base of her neck. He cupped her breast, using his thumb and forefinger to squeeze her nipple.

Gasping, she dug her fingers into his scalp. "Isn't it too soon to do this again?"

"Not for me. I'm more than ready." He tipped his head up and looked into her blue eyes. "However, if you aren't, that's all right."

"Do what you did to my breast again."

He pinched her—not hard—then tugged on the nipple. "That?"

"Yes." The word hissed from her lips as her eyes slitted. "I am also ready. Now."

"We needn't hurry." He bent his head to her breast and put his mouth where his thumb and finger had been. He licked and sucked, drawing soft, arousing whimpers from her.

Suddenly, she pushed him to his back and came over him. The pale globes of her breasts swung before his gaze, taunting him, the peaks pink and turgid.

"We've all night," she said huskily. "I want to try as many things as possible. That night in the library, you put your mouth on me. I want to do the same to you."

He'd already been aroused, but now a white-hot lust careened through him. Blood rushed to his cock, lengthening it even more. "Briefly," he said, his voice sounding strained. "I don't think I can stand more than that."

Her brow creased. "Is it painful? I would have thought it would feel as good as when you did it to me?"

"Oh, it does," he assured her. "The problem is that it feels too good, and then I'll spend myself sooner than I'd like. With each release, it takes me a little longer to recover."

"I see. Well, you'll have to tell me what to do and when to stop." She pushed the bedclothes back behind her and braced her hands on his chest, using her fingers and palms to explore every inch of his bare flesh. By the time, she reached his waist, he was practically panting.

Repeating what she'd done earlier, she wrapped her hand around him and stroked his length. But after a few passes, she went lower, her hand cupping his balls. "Should I touch these?"

"You can," he croaked, fearful that he would embarrass himself in short order, and she hadn't even taken him in her mouth. "Be gentle," he said. "They aren't as forgiving as the shaft."

"That is very good to know." She pulled her hand up to the tip, and as she descended once more, her head lowered. The plait was nearly gone now, and her thick, wavy red hair grazed his thighs.

He held his breath as she drew back his foreskin and pressed her lips to the tip. Gripping the base, she opened her mouth and took him onto her tongue, then closed her lips around him.

Though he'd wanted to watch her, his eyes slammed closed, and his head fell back as an unparalleled ecstasy swept over him. "Yes, Rebecca. Just like that." He cupped her nape as she moved over him, slowly at first.

With great effort, he willed himself to hold on. He didn't want to come yet. If he hadn't done so earlier, it would likely already have been over.

He managed to open one eye and watch her suck him. It was the most erotic thing he'd ever seen. She moved faster and swirled her tongue around him with each stroke.

"Enough," he rasped, tugging on her head. "Ride me."

She looked up at him, her lips red and wet. "Do what?"

"Straddle my hips. You're going to be on top and take control this time. But kiss me first. Now. Please."

When she was positioned over him, her sex pressed against his, she leaned down. He pulled her toward him, his lips crashing into hers. Their mouths met, open and wet, tongues clashing. He lifted his hips, rotating his pelvis against hers. She ground down, and desire pulsed from his cock to every part of him.

He put his hand between them, and she did the same. They met at his cock, and together guided him into her sheath. She was as wet as before, more than ready. He hated thinking of all the lonely years of her marriage when her idiot husband hadn't realized he'd been married to an actual goddess. No, he wouldn't think of that. Not now. She was his. For tonight, at least.

He thrust up as she pushed down. She tore her mouth from his and cried out his name, moving her hands to his shoulders. He reached for one of her glorious breasts, then lifted his head from the bed to suckle her.

Her muscles tightened around him as he drew on her nipple. She moved faster, her sheath gripping him with each stroke. He was helpless to do anything but fall back and let her find a rhythm.

Her hips pitched forward so she could rub her clitoris against him. He watched her ride him like that, her movements growing more frenzied until he knew she was close. Slipping his hand between them once more, he stroked her hard and fast. She bore down, her sheath a delicious vise about his cock.

Her cries filled the room as her body went rigid and then shook with her orgasm. It was a stunning vision to behold, her head cast back, her throat a long, pale column he longed to kiss and lick. He wanted to own every single part of her.

The orgasm he'd kept at bay rushed at him, and he had to clasp her hips to pull her off him. "Sorry," he murmured, just barely separating them before he spurted his release.

Encircling his cock with his hand, he finished himself. Then her hand curled around his, joining him as he spent what remained.

She lay next to him, and it was several minutes until their breathing became somewhat regular. He'd never encountered a woman who'd given so much of herself, especially someone with what was apparently limited experience. Her husband had been the biggest of fools.

He turned to her and kissed her gently. "You are beautiful in every way. Thank you for a night I will never forget."

"We're finished?" She sounded rather disappointed.

Nash chuckled. "For now. We both need a bit of recovery."

"I suppose that makes sense." She yawned as she snuggled against him, her soft, warm body fitting into his as if they'd been crafted to be one. "I am tired."

"Sleep," he whispered, brushing her hair back

from her face and kissing her temple. "I will be here when you wake."

She looked him in the eye. "I'm counting on it."

~

*A*s promised, Nash had been there when Rebecca had woken before dawn. It was a silly thing to be so pleased about, but Horatio had always left her bed, from the very start of their marriage. She hadn't really minded since she'd found no pleasure in his arms, but since she had experienced considerable pleasure with Nash, she didn't want him to go.

And he hadn't. He'd awakened her with his mouth on her sex, bringing her to the brink of release before turning her over and taking her from behind. That had been an astonishing orgasm. Her legs had quivered for some time after.

They'd enjoyed a lovely breakfast together in his sitting room, during which it had rained on and off again. Nash had once again offered the use of his coach to transport her to Black Sheep Farm.

"But I don't need to accompany you," he said. "I will if you want, but I'll understand if this is something you need to do alone."

Perhaps it was the night they'd spent together, but Rebecca felt close to him and was glad for his support. "I'd like if you came with me." She glanced toward the window. "Particularly since I'm fairly certain I will need your coach."

"And you shall have it." He'd smiled at her, and somehow, it made her even more giddy than his smiles before last night. It was as if everything between them had intensified—in the very best way.

The coachman met them in the common room, and Rebecca gave him directions to Black Sheep

Farm. Then they dashed for the coach since the rain was coming down in buckets.

As the rain hammered the top of the carriage and sluiced down the windows, Rebecca moved closer against Nash's side. Unlike their other trips in the coach, she didn't bother trying to keep her distance. He clasped her hand, and Rebecca couldn't help but smile. This was what she'd hoped her marriage might be. An easy camaraderie, a shared comfort.

"I appreciate you coming with me," she said.

"You aren't nervous, are you?" He stroked his thumb along her hand.

"A little. Not as much as I was seeing Leah. If my mother were still at the farm, I would be more than nervous. I'd be terrified."

"It's a good thing she won't be there, because I wouldn't be able to withhold my opinion of her treatment of you and your siblings, especially Leah."

She looked over at his face. His brows were pitched low, his mouth set in a ferocious near snarl. "You look like an angry badger."

He blinked at her. "A badger? I'm not sure I know what to make of that comparison. Aren't they some-what…cute? I saw one when I was young, and I re-member thinking its stripes were charming."

Giggling, she said, "You wouldn't say that if you'd encountered one that was upset. It was squaring off with one of our goats."

"Who won?"

"Neither. Barn, my brother, chased the badger off with a stick."

"You say your brother still lives at the farm?"

She nodded. "He will take it over from our father one day. He and his family live in a cottage on the farm, though in the last letter I received from his wife, it sounded as though they may move into the larger house while my father takes the cottage."

They were silent a few minutes as the coach left town and passed farmland. At length, Nash said, "Listening to your badger story, it seemed your childhood held at least a few pleasant memories."

"It did. I'm just ashamed to say that very few of them included Leah. She was always given more chores than us, and when she was allowed to leave the house, she nearly always went to the botanical gardens or to Radford Grange. To be with Phin. Once they became friends—I think she was around six, perhaps—she was eager to spend time with him. Not just him, but his family. They made her feel welcome. I remember there was a time when Phin's grandfather came to ask if they could take Leah into their household. He'd made the offer kindly, saying he only wished to ease our family's burden. That infuriated our mother. She…hurt Leah so that she wasn't able to leave the house for at least a fortnight."

Nash's dark eyes rounded. "What do you mean she hurt her?"

"She used to hit Leah, but never where anyone would see. That time, she hit her in the face, so Leah couldn't leave the farm."

"What a rotten, coldhearted person," he muttered before his gaze softened. "How did such a warmhearted person such as you come from her?"

"You think I'm warmhearted? How can you know that about me?"

He gave her an encouraging smile. "Seeing you with your sister and witnessing the hurt you bore for so many years, it's impossible to think you are anything else."

She hadn't ever thought of herself that way. Hearing him say it made her feel…light, as if she could be the person she wanted and hoped to be. "Thank you."

The coach slowed, and Rebecca looked out the

window as they turned up the drive to the farm. She tensed, and Nash's grip on her hand tightened. He leaned over and kissed her cheek. "You've already been through the hard part," he said softly.

He was right. If this went half as well as things had gone with Leah, Rebecca had no reason to be concerned. Still, the mind would do what it would, and hers apparently wanted to be anxious.

When the coach came to a stop, Nash met her gaze. "Do you want me to come with you, or should I wait here?"

"Come with me. Please." She hadn't realized how much it had meant to have him at her side when she'd gone to dinner at Radford Grange, but looking back, she wasn't sure she could have managed it alone.

The rain had lessened to a faint drizzle. Nash helped her to the ground, and they hurried to the front door. Seeing the house after nearly a decade made her throat constrict. There were so many memories, and coming here brought them all to the fore—the good and especially the bad.

Nash knocked on the door, and they heard the sound of running feet. Then, "Jacob Webster, don't you open that door! Get back to your reading!"

A woman opened the door a moment later. She was in her forties and wore a sparkling white apron and a matching cap, beneath which dark curls were barely visible. "Good morning," she said somewhat warily.

Rebecca summoned a smile. "Good morning. I'm Mrs. Sweet. I'm here to see Mr. Webster."

Before the woman could respond, another woman came to the door. She smiled broadly as she wiped her hands on her apron that was not quite as snowy white as the older woman's. "Rebecca!" Dorothea Webster, whom they all called Thea, exclaimed. "I heard you were in town. Come in, come in."

The older woman held the door as Rebecca stepped over the threshold, followed by Nash.

Rebecca gestured to him. "Allow me to present my employer, the Marquess of Creslow." Except he wasn't her employer any longer. But how else was she to introduce him? As her lover? Her friend? Her former employer?

Employer seemed easiest.

If Nash found her introduction odd, he didn't reflect it. He smiled grandly at both women, and Rebecca wondered if they would melt beneath the onslaught of his charms as she had. Goodness, she hoped not. She didn't need her own family fawning over him. The swarm of young ladies at the festival was bad enough.

Was she jealous?

She hadn't thought so until that moment, but yes, it seemed she was.

The older woman dipped a curtsey. "Good morning, my lord."

Thea did the same, then presented the woman who'd answered the door. "This is our housekeeper, Mrs. Perkins. She also helps with the children, thank goodness."

"They have three," Rebecca said to Nash. "Two boys and a girl." She looked to her sister-in-law. "I am hoping to meet them." *Meet* them. Why had she not seen any of her family in nearly a decade? Had avoiding her mother been worth that loss? She suddenly felt angry—at her mother and at herself.

"Mrs. Perkins can fetch them shortly. I imagine you want to see Barn. And your father. As it happens, I saw them coming toward the house."

The familiar sounds of the rear door into the

kitchen creaking and slamming shut met Rebecca's ears. "The kitchen door still makes that noise."

"Yes," Thea said with an eye roll. "We just moved in last week, but it's on my list of things that need to be repaired."

"You did swap houses with Father, then?" Rebecca asked.

"It made sense with our growing family." Thea touched her belly. "I've another coming by Christmas. And your father is on his own now, which I think he likes, by the way." She lowered her voice. "We all like that—her being gone, I mean."

Again, there was no need to specify who *her* was.

"Who're you talking to, Mill?"

Rebecca recognized her brother's voice. She blew out a breath and glanced at Nash. He gave her a supportive nod that calmed her racing heart.

"You won't believe who's here," Thea called back to him, smiling.

Then Barnabas came from the dining room, his hat in his hand. He looked the same, but different, older of course. His hair was receding from his forehead, but the dark mop was still thick. He grinned upon seeing her. "Becky Bex."

That was what her father had called her. He'd assigned similar nicknames to her brother and one sister: Barney Barn and Maggie Meg. But not for Leah.

Montford Webster stepped out from behind Barn, who was several inches taller. Her father's blond hair had given way to a great deal of white, and the jowls of his cheeks hung lower. He was also wearing spectacles.

"It *is* Becky Bex!" their father exclaimed, beaming as he saw her.

The depth of his reaction—the excitement evidenced in his expression—gave her pause. She didn't know how to react. While he'd never been cruel like

her mother, he also hadn't been particularly demonstrative. The nicknames he'd given them were, if not
the only, then the greatest indication that he'd cared
for his children. Well, three of them anyway. It was
worth remembering that he hadn't used them within
earshot of their mother.

"Careful, Papa, you're scaring her," Barn said with
a chuckle.

Their father nodded, his features sobering. "It's
been a long time." Were those tears in his eyes behind
the spectacles? "I hope I don't scare you, my girl. I'm
just pleased to see you."

"I can see that," Rebecca responded softly. "I'm
just not used to that." She didn't care to be gentle
with her observations or remarks. That time was
past.

"No, I suppose you wouldn't be." Her father
sniffed. "I don't know if you wish to discuss anything
from…before, but things are different here now that
your mother is gone. We don't hide our feelings, especially our joy."

"That *is* a change," Rebecca murmured. "So long
as Leah is welcome here and treated well, I'd probably prefer to leave the past where it belongs."

Barn looked her in the eye. "That's what I said.
Still, I apologized to Leah."

Rebecca saw the same pain in his gaze that she'd
carried for so long. "I did too."

"We did what we thought we had to," Barn said,
his voice weighted with regret.

"Don't any of you people hug one another?" Nash
asked with some much-needed humor.

Everyone looked at him, and Rebecca hurriedly
introduced him.

Nash shook Rebecca's father's hand. "I'm so
pleased to meet you, Mr. Webster." He turned to
Barn. "And you, Mr. Webster."

"I heard you were working for a nobleman as a matchmaker," her father said. "I imagine a matchmaker hailing from Marrywell would be in high demand."

Rebecca blinked at him. "Actually, I hadn't used that as a way to advertise my services, but perhaps I should."

Her father grinned. "Once you match the marquess this week, I daresay you won't need to. Everyone will want to hire the Marrywell Matchmaker."

Perhaps if that had any chance of happening, which it did not since Nash had changed his mind. Besides, the thought of matching him with anyone turned Rebecca's stomach. It was a good thing he'd terminated her employment, for if he hadn't, she would have had to resign after last night. Except last night wouldn't have happened if not for her dismissal.

"I'll fetch the children so they can meet their aunt," Thea said before departing.

"Come into the parlor," Rebecca's father beckoned, moving into the room from the entry hall. Barn followed him, but Rebecca didn't move.

Nash came up beside her, his hand grazing her lower back. "Is something wrong?" he whispered.

"We weren't allowed in that room." Rebecca and Meg had played in there once when they thought their mother had gone into town, which she didn't do very often. Only, she'd come home because she'd forgotten something and had caught them disobeying her. They'd been given bread for dinner for a week.

"It looks as though you are now."

"As much as I say I don't want to look backward, it's impossible not to since I returned to Marrywell. Especially here." Her gaze found his. "Thank you for being with me. It helps."

"I'm glad." He looked at her mouth, and she had the distinct impression he wanted to kiss her.

Later.

She hoped.

"Walk with me," Nash said quietly as he applied a slight pressure on her back.

Taking the first step toward the parlor, Rebecca willed herself to be strong. She was no longer a child. She was a different person from the girl who'd left Marrywell with her husband. It seemed as though everyone else had changed too.

Thea returned with the children, and Rebecca happily met her two nephews and niece, a precocious toddler who climbed right onto Rebecca's lap. Her auburn hair smelled of lavender soap, and she fixated on the gold-colored buttons of Rebecca's spencer.

"I'd say she likes you," Barn said with a laugh. "But she wants to sit on everyone's lap." He looked to Nash. "Careful, you may be next."

Rebecca shot a glance toward Nash to see his reaction. He smiled, but his eyes were inscrutable.

"Is there any chance you're staying longer than the festival?" her father asked.

"I'm considering it." Rebecca couldn't deny that she wanted to spend more time with her family now that things were different. Perhaps they'd all be able to find happiness or even love with one another.

"Stay, Aunt Rebecca," Jacob, her oldest nephew who was six, said. "You need to come back and meet Hal."

"Hal is his dog," Thea clarified. "He is outside while Jacob works on his lessons. The day school is closed this week for the festival."

"I shall definitely need to meet Hal," Rebecca assured him.

They visited for a while longer, and Rebecca relaxed enough that she even laughed at a few memories Barn shared, including one in which the two of them had stolen into the brewer's field and swiped two bottles of ale. They'd both been incredibly ill and had lied about the cause—too much pudding from the pudding competition. Their father laughed with them before sobering to say he was sorry they hadn't been able to tell the truth, that he would not have punished them. While that might have been true, their mother had ruled the roost, and punishment would have been swift and harsh.

They said their goodbyes and planned to see each other at the Grand Picnic, which was in the middle of the festival.

As she and Nash made their way back to his coach, he sent her a smile. "That went well. Your family is charming."

"*Now.* I'm having a hard time reconciling the past with the present." She grimaced, wishing this wasn't so difficult.

"It will take time, I suspect." He helped her into the coach and directed the coachman to return to the inn. "You enjoyed yourself, didn't you?" he asked as he settled himself beside her on the seat.

"I did, actually. Especially with the children." She smiled, thinking of how lovely it felt to have Abby on her lap.

The carriage started moving as he looked over at her. "Did you want children?"

"I did. Very much." It had been almost an ache. "I suppose I wanted the chance to be a better mother than mine."

"I can understand that." His gaze was fixed forward now, his voice sounding almost distant.

Rebecca fidgeted a moment as she contemplated whether to tell him something. In the end, the words tumbled forth of their own accord. "Last night, after the first time we were together...when I realized why you'd left me, I felt a little sad." She watched his brows form a V as he snapped his attention toward her and rushed to add, "Not that I was expecting to have a child with you. I wanted one—before. Did you want children? I mean, I know your duty seems to require that, but that isn't the same as wanting them, is it?"

"No, it isn't."

She noted he didn't answer the first question. "Would you like to have children?"

"It doesn't really matter since I need to have them. Or at least one who is male." He sounded cool, not at all the passionate, caring man she'd come to know.

"I've been incredibly open with you the past few days, exposing myself in ways I never have. Because you were kind and supportive. Have I not been that to you?"

"You have," he answered slowly, almost re-luctantly.

"Then why won't you reveal yourself to me the way I have to you?"

"Because I don't do that." He didn't snap at her ex-actly, but neither was his response pleasant. "With anyone. Please don't take it personally."

How could she not?

The happiness she'd felt all morning, even amidst the anxiety of seeing her family again, dimmed. She reminded herself that she'd only agreed to one night with him, that all this was temporary even if it lasted a day or three longer.

Sharing a marvelous night together changed nothing. They would go their separate ways soon enough. In the meantime, she could enjoy this fleeting affair. Or she could end things right now.

CHAPTER 10

*H*ad he really just told Rebecca not to take his obnoxious behavior personally? Nash cringed inwardly. He was behaving like an utter shit.

How could she *not* take his lack of disclosure personally? She had opened herself up to him in every way possible, and he continued to hold her at arm's length. While claiming to want to be her friend.

They were much more than that now, weren't they?

He wasn't sure. No, that wasn't the answer he wanted. He didn't *wish* to be more than friends who were also temporary lovers.

Revealing himself emotionally made him vulnerable, and he hadn't done that since Louisa. He couldn't lower his guard that completely. The devastation of her loss had been absolute. So much so that he'd been certain there would be no possibility for him to feel an inkling of anything for anyone ever again.

Yet here he was. With inklings.

For a woman who'd suffered enough people treating her poorly. Did he really want to be one of their number?

He hadn't intended to respond to her query, but

the words suddenly fell from his mouth. "Yes, I wanted children." His voice sounded unusual to his ears. Or perhaps it was just the fact that he was saying that out loud to someone. "But my wife became ill very soon after we wed. She died eighteen months into the marriage."

Now Rebecca was the one to take his hand, holding it in his lap. "I'm so sorry. I sense you loved her very much."

"Er, yes." He shifted, discomfort making him want to flee. Not from Rebecca, but from the pain of thinking about these things, especially in the presence of another person. Particularly in the presence of someone about whom he cared, in spite of everything. "I don't like discussing her or that time."

"I imagine that's painful. Very recently, someone helped me face something in my past that was painful. Things have worked out—so far—surprisingly well. Have you considered it may be time to discuss her and that time?" She spoke gently, with great care.

He recognized that she was only trying to help. Still, the notion that what he'd endured with Louisa, who'd *died*, could compare to what Rebecca had gone through in her youth seemed incomparable to him. And didn't that make him an even bigger shit?

Wiping his free hand over his face, he struggled to dispel the frightful agitation building within him. It had been years since he'd completely given in to the emotions of loss and grief and anger. At least he'd had a brief period of joy with Louisa. Some people, including the woman holding his hand, weren't fortunate enough to experience even that. At least, she hadn't yet.

This was all too much. He managed to take a deep breath and forced himself to respond to her question. "I have considered that, but I have found there is little point. Unlike with your situation, there is nothing to heal, no hope for a relationship in the future. That is a part of my life that is over and finished. There's really nothing to be said."

The darkness hovered over him. He had to keep it from stalling and engulfing him completely. Summoning a smile, he lifted Rebecca's hand to his lips and kissed the gloved back. "You are so kind to care for me. Don't you think we'll be remiss if we don't use our remaining time in the carriage to do something we won't speak of later?"

She arched a brow. "Whatever happens in the carriage stays in the carriage?"

"Just so." He began to relax, particularly when the fire of desire lit her eyes.

"There isn't much time."

"Lift your skirts and straddle my lap." He began to unfasten his fall. His cock was already hard, which seemed slightly miraculous given how he'd been feeling a few moments before.

But Rebecca stirred him in ways no one had.

Wait, not even Louisa?

That had been different. They'd shared a brilliant love. With Rebecca, he'd felt an instant passion for her the moment they'd met. It had persisted even after they'd parted, then roared back when he'd made her reacquaintance the other day. When he was with her, he wanted more—more of her, more time, more everything.

And that was utterly terrifying.

She settled herself over him, her gaze meeting his. There were no words as he guided his cock into her wet sheath, but there was still a flow of communication between them. They shared desire and need, and a silent acknowledgment that this was something special and unique.

Holding his gaze as she sank completely down his

shaft, she gripped the side of his neck and his shoulder. He held her waist, digging his fingers into her as his cock swelled within her. The motion of the coach created a friction. Then she began to move, increasing it.

They should find their release quickly, but he was absolutely entranced with her. She controlled the pace, rising and falling with a delicious precision. Then she finally broke eye contact, and he suddenly wanted to drive relentlessly into her until she broke apart.

She leaned forward and brushed her lips against his jaw. "Make me come," she whispered against his ear. "Now."

Nash let go, thrusting up as he held her tightly in his grip. After several strokes, he moved his hand between them and found her clitoris. A moment later, her muscles clenched around him, and she cast her head back, crying out as she orgasmed like a torrential storm.

He felt his own release building to its climax. He moved his other hand back to her waist to lift her away from him.

"Don't come," she commanded.

Fighting to do as she said, he closed his eyes and tried to breathe. When her shudders calmed, she pulled herself away from him. Then he felt her mouth close around him.

His eyes flew open. He looked down at her kneeling on the floor of the coach, her head between his legs as she sucked his cock. He'd already been close. He was absolutely going to come in her mouth. Did she know that?

He clasped her head. "Rebecca, I'm going to spill in your mouth if you don't stop."

She glanced up, her eyes expectant. Her mouth only moved faster.

Nash closed his eyes once more and surrendered to this astonishing woman. She'd known he couldn't finish inside her, and in this moment, she'd wanted to nurture his completion.

His orgasm swept over him, his hips coming off the seat as his muscles went rigid. He had two thoughts. One, Rebecca was an absolute gift.

Two, this was dangerous. He should leave before things could progress any further.

~

Though Rebecca had spent the afternoon catching up on the sleep she'd missed with last night's activities and taking a warm, restorative bath, before dining and preparing for the evening, she still felt anxious. Because of Nash.

Earlier, in the coach, she'd pressed him to share more of himself. At first, she didn't think he was going to do it, but then he'd surprised her by sharing what had happened, albeit sparingly, with his wife.

Then he'd shocked her further by turning to their mutual physical attraction. As much as she'd wanted to hear more from him on the topic of his wife and his desire for children and pretty much anything he wished to share, she'd been helpless to resist his seductive prowess.

Or, she'd simply wanted to be close to him after he'd opened up to her, even a little.

She knew it was the latter. She was becoming rather…fond of him. That probably wasn't an adequate description, but she didn't think it would be wise to allow herself to think of anything else.

At least not yet.

She would take their friendship, affair, liaison, whatever he wanted to call it, as slowly as possible. That was clearly best for him, and it was for her too.

She'd utterly failed at love so far, and she wasn't sure she trusted that she was meant for that emotion.

A maid came to remove the remains of her small dinner, and Rebecca went into her dressing room to put on her jasper necklace, the only gift that Horatio had ever given her. She wouldn't even bother wearing it, but it was the only jewelry she owned besides her gold wedding band, and *that* she refused to wear.

The red stone complemented her ivory gown trimmed with scarlet ribbon. She'd wondered whether she ought to wear a ball gown to the brewer's field and had decided she would likely have nowhere else to wear it this week since they would not be attending most of the festival events.

A knock on her door prompted her to grab her gloves and take one final look in the mirror before walking back into her bedchamber. Rebecca hesitated as she pulled on a glove. It would be Nash, but which door had he knocked on? The one they shared had been conspicuously unused all afternoon and so far this early evening.

Conspicuously? Did she think last night meant they would come and go from each other's rooms without concern?

She tugged on her other glove and decided he would be at the door leading to the corridor. Smoothing her hands along the skirt of her gown as she made her way there, she took a deep breath before opening it.

And there he was. Absolutely resplendent in an ebony suit of clothing and a...red waistcoat. They matched.

His gaze swept over her. "The red is lovely," he said with a faint smirk.

"I would say the same to you."

He didn't offer her his arm, and she couldn't decide if that was strange. The other day, she'd established that, as his employee, she wouldn't be taking his arm. Only, she wasn't his employee any longer.

Perhaps he was feeling anxious like she was. But was it for the same reasons?

Rebecca doubted that was possible. She summoned a smile and worked to put her uncertain thoughts away, at least for this evening. She wanted to enjoy her time at the festival.

As they descended the stairs, he asked, "Should we take the coach in case we overimbibe and walking proves an insurmountable challenge?"

Laughing, Rebecca shook her head. "I hope not. I can't imagine that level of overindulgence would allow for a pleasant tomorrow."

"You've a point," he responded with a smile.

"Besides, it looks as though the weather cleared up very nicely this afternoon. I do hope the sky remains clear."

"That would be lovely, particularly since I didn't notice the brewer's field having a tent or any other cover."

"They do erect a tent if the weather is poor, so I expect they did that earlier today. They may have even done it last night."

He opened the door for her, and they walked toward the street. The High Street was filled with people moving toward the gardens. They had to slow as they waited to pass through the gate. Inside, hundreds of people milled about in the fine evening air.

"This is much nicer than being in the assembly rooms," he said.

"I think so. There's just something magically beautiful about the botanical gardens during the matchmaking festival. Perhaps it's all the love floating in the air." Knowing how Nash felt about that emotion, Rebecca wondered if she shouldn't have said that.

They made their way to the brewer's field, which was also crowded. They stopped at the first booth. Rebecca knew the brewer—Jeremiah Barstow. She'd had a tendre for him for a year or so when she'd been fourteen, but he'd been twenty and far too old for her. He was very attractive, with bright blue eyes and thick, sandy brown hair. She noted his athletic form had somewhat deteriorated, and he now sported a belly that indicated he enjoyed drinking his ale as much as he did crafting it. He was also married with at least one child.

Looking past Nash, Jeremiah's gaze landed on Rebecca. His lips spread in a broad smile, his blue eyes crinkling at the corners. "If it isn't Beautiful Becky." He held his hand out to her, and Rebecca had no choice but to offer hers.

She smiled at him. "It's good to see you, Jem."

He brought her hand to his lips and pressed a kiss to the back of her glove. "As beautiful as ever. I daresay, even more so. And you're a widow, I hear?"

"I am."

"I am sorry for your loss. Even more, for your husband's. Poor fellow to have to leave you!" He laughed as he released her hand.

Rebecca gestured to Nash. "Allow me to present the Marquess of Creslow."

Jeremiah narrowed his eyes at Nash. "I've heard of you. I hope you're finding our festival to your liking." He gave Nash a confident nod. "I'll pour my best ale for you."

He asked one of his young helpers to provide two tankards of ale, then turned back to Rebecca. "I'll look for you later." He winked at her.

Rebecca could only imagine what Jem might have in mind. His lingering stares, with several glances toward her bodice, along with his comment on her being a widow indicated a potentially salacious interest.

A young man handed them their ale, and Rebecca thanked him and Jem, preferring not to address Jem's comment. Turning, she asked Nash where he'd like to sit.

"I don't see anything," he said, looking out over the crowded field. There were two tents set up on the opposite side, with long tables beneath them.

"I see available seats under the tents. People are likely choosing to sit in the open air since the weather is finally fair."

"Come," Nash said, gently clasping her elbow.

She snapped her attention toward him, slightly surprised that he was touching her after not yet doing so this evening. But it was very close with so many people jostling about them, and he was likely just trying to ensure they stayed together.

He guided her to an empty spot at the end of one of the tables. She squeezed onto the bench while he sat opposite her and immediately took a sip of ale.

"Jem makes excellent ale," she remarked, taking another sip.

"Jem also has an eye for you," Nash said, peering at her over the rim of his tankard before he drank.

"He's married," she pointed out. "Not that that stops some people from behaving inappropriately."

"If he bothers you, I'll take care of him." Nash's dark eyes glittered with promise.

"Thank you." Rebecca smiled, glad to have his support.

"Rebecca?"

The tentative feminine voice prompted Rebecca to look up. Two women had arrived at the end of their table. Rebecca recognized one of them. "Teresa?" Teresa Albright had been a friend of Rebecca's.

Her father's farm wasn't far from Black Sheep Farm. Rebecca didn't know the other woman.

Teresa beamed. "Yes, that's right. How splendid to see you after so long. I thought you might never return to Marrywell. This is my cousin, Helen." Teresa, who was the same age as Rebecca, flicked a glance toward Nash.

Rebecca inclined her head toward him. "Allow me to present the Marquess of Creslow."

Teresa curtseyed to Nash, and Helen, who was several years younger than her cousin, with shining blonde hair and rich, chocolate-brown eyes, also curtseyed.

"I heard you are his matchmaker," Teresa said.

Helen blushed prettily. "Pleased to meet you, my lord."

Oh no. Was Teresa hoping Rebecca might help her cousin? Or herself? Rebecca looked to see if Teresa was wearing a wedding ring, but she had gloves on.

Teresa smiled at Rebecca before speaking to Nash. "We were searching for a place to sit. Do you mind if we slide onto the bench?"

"Not at all." Nash scooted over. Instead of sitting down beside him, Teresa indicated for Helen to do that. Then Teresa turned to Rebecca.

Realizing the new arrivals couldn't sit down when seats were quickly becoming scarce, Rebecca slid over to allow space for Teresa to sit beside her.

"Thank you," Teresa said to her before focusing her attention on Nash. "How are you enjoying our festival here in Marrywell?"

"It's certainly unlike anything I've ever experienced." He lifted his tankard. "You don't have any ale."

Helen made a slight face, which did nothing to detract from her loveliness. "I don't care for it."

"I may fetch a tankard in a bit," Teresa said. "Where did you get yours?" she asked, nodding toward Nash's tankard.

"Jeremiah Barstow," Rebecca answered.

"Oh, Jem! His ale is wonderful. It's my husband's favorite." Teresa was married, then.

Rebecca deduced that this must be an effort to match her cousin with Nash. She leaned toward her old friend and spoke in a whisper. "I'm afraid his lordship has decided against marrying for the time being. In case you were hoping he might take an interest in your cousin."

Teresa turned her head toward Rebecca, her gray eyes widening. "Oh, that's too bad. Well, it can't hurt for her to become acquainted with him."

"I suppose not." Rebecca's jaw tightened. She didn't particularly want to share Nash. She wanted whatever time she had with him to be uninterrupted —by marriage-minded ladies or discomfort such as Nash had experienced that afternoon in the coach. She much preferred more of what had happened after that. If all she would have was a series of delightful memories of being in his arms, she would take that.

But if she were honest, she wanted more.

She wanted his attention fully on her.

"Do you like the ale, my lord?" Helen asked.

"I do," he said. "You may sample mine, if you like." He slid his tankard toward the young beauty.

She batted her lashes like a skilled coquette. "That's generous of you." She managed to hoist the tankard daintily, as if she were picking up a teacup and pursed her lips upon the rim. All of them watched as she took a small sip. Her brows shot up as she set the tankard back upon the table. "That's somewhat…bitter."

"It's not the most bitter I've tasted," Rebecca said,

and although she was referring to the ale, she realized it could mean a great many things. This very situation was making her extremely bitter.

Then salvation arrived in the form of the May Queen herself. "Leah!" Rebecca called out, drawing Leah to turn. Phin was beside her, but engaged in conversation with someone else. She stood on her toes and whispered in his ear before coming toward Rebecca.

Rebecca slid to the other end of the bench, which would hold one more person, and rose. "Please excuse me," she said to Nash and the ladies before hurrying to intercept Leah.

"Oh," Leah said in surprise as Rebecca blocked her path from the table. "I was going to say good evening to Creslow."

"He's engaged with Teresa Albright or whatever her name is now and her young, *beautiful* cousin, Helen."

Leah nodded slowly. "I see. Let us take a short promenade, then." She threaded her arm through Rebecca's. "Though that may be difficult amidst this crush."

"Let's just go over here," Rebecca said, guiding them to the hedge, which served as the exterior wall of the brewer's field.

"I take it you didn't want to sit with Creslow and his admirers?" Leah asked. "I assume that's what they are."

"Something like that. Teresa was hoping Helen might catch Nash's eye. However, I informed her that he's changed his mind about marrying, at least for the moment."

"Has he?" Leah frowned slightly. "That will cause a stir. He was among the most sought-after bachelors in attendance, of course, especially since I think the

Earl of Gilbourne has departed. Why has the marquess changed his mind?"

Rebecca considered whether to share the truth. It would be so nice to confide in someone. She'd never had that. She looked over at the table where Nash sat with Teresa and Helen. The latter sat so close to him that their arms touched. He was speaking, and the ladies were listening, rapt. Suddenly, they laughed, while Nash grinned before lifting his tankard for a drink.

Jerking her attention to Leah, Rebecca decided she *needed* a confidante. "Between us, he wasn't even looking for a 'real' wife. He needs a marchioness and an heir to fulfill his duty. He wants a business arrangement without love. Once I learned that was his goal, I explained how difficult it may be to attain that at this festival where love matches are both the norm and expected." Rebecca hesitated to reveal the rest, that she'd had her own reservations about facilitating a marriage that wasn't based on love. She hadn't even told Nash that, and she didn't have to since he'd terminated her employment.

Leah blew out a breath. "People do attend the festival to find love. He's postponed looking for a wife, then?"

"Yes, he terminated my employment." Rebecca stopped just short of explaining his reasoning behind that and her subsequent surrender to temptation.

"I'm sorry to hear that," Leah said, touching her arm.

"I am concerned it may reflect poorly on my abilities, but Nash has assured me that he'll write a letter of recommendation for future clients."

"You keep calling him Nash. I suppose you've become close working together?" Leah gave her a pointed look. "Close enough that you took him to Black Sheep Farm this morning?"

Rebecca shrugged, hoping Leah wouldn't detect there was more between them. "He offered his coach since it was raining. I didn't want to be rude and not invite him. Who told you?"

"Thea. I saw her a little while ago when we arrived at the gardens."

Rebecca had returned to watching Nash and the ladies at the table. A third, unknown woman was now sitting down on his other side. He was smiling and laughing, seeming to have a lovely time. The unknown woman leaned close to him and spoke near his ear. He turned his head toward her, and for a brief moment, Rebecca wondered if they might kiss. But they didn't. They merely engaged in what looked to be an intimate conversation. Rebecca's hands and neck felt suddenly clammy.

"He reminds me of your husband, with all the women fawning over him," Leah said. "Horatio Sweet was quite popular at the festival. I was glad when he chose you."

"I was too," Rebecca murmured. "But I was incredibly wrong about him. His behavior at the festival wasn't real." She'd taken a chance in order to get away from Black Sheep Farm, and she'd hoped the marriage would be loving and fruitful. How had she endured so many years with him? Looking back, she wasn't sure how she'd managed.

Leah gazed at her with sympathy. "I'm sorry you weren't happy. Perhaps you'll find love again. Plenty of widows find happiness. Just last year, a widow I was acquainted with from London fell in love and married. Indeed, they've returned this year to celebrate their unexpected joy."

Again. As if Rebecca had ever found love. "I don't expect that for myself," Rebecca said stiffly. She was suddenly overcome with emotion and had to swallow and blink to stop a tear from falling.

Looking at her sister, she earnestly asked, "How did you do it? How did you manage to love Phin in spite of everything? How did you even know what love looked or felt like?"

Pressing her lips together, Leah took a moment to respond. "I'm not sure. I just know that Phin was always in my heart, first as a dear friend, then as something I couldn't describe because I was too young, really, and finally as a romantic partner, though I never thought he'd reciprocate my feelings."

"Is that why you left Marrywell?"

"Partly, but it was mostly because I just had to get away from Black Sheep Farm. You know. You did the same thing."

Rebecca nodded, her throat tight.

Leah touched Rebecca's arm again, rubbing the upper portion. "You've felt love, whether you know it or not. Remember the baby goat you practically raised? You clearly loved her."

A laugh bubbled from Rebecca's throat. "I did love Marigold. Perhaps I'm not as broken as I thought." Because she did want love, and she thought she was beginning to recognize it. Watching Nash with the other women made her feel queasy, and it wasn't simply a jealous reaction. She wanted the attention he was giving them because she wanted to give it back to him. She wanted to share every moment they could. Was that love?

It didn't matter because he refused to love. She needed to end their affair as soon as possible before she lost her heart completely.

"We're all a little fractured," Leah said, giving Rebecca's arm a squeeze before dropping her hand with a warm smile. "And we have each other to help keep the pieces together."

They did. Now. "I've never had that. Phin said I could come stay with you at Radford Grange. I'd like to stay for the rest of the festival and perhaps a bit longer. Would you mind?"

Leah grinned. "I would be thrilled. Stay as long as you like."

"Thank you." Relief worked its way through Rebecca, loosening her shoulders. Whatever happened, she had something she hadn't before returning to Marrywell—she had her family. She caught sight of Jem coming toward them and leaned toward Leah.

Rebecca clutched her sister's hand. "Jeremiah Barstow is heading straight for us. Please don't leave me alone with him."

"Why not? I thought you liked him. But then, that was another lifetime, wasn't it?"

Indeed it was. "He was being rather...suggestive earlier."

Leah's eyes rounded. "But he's married!"

"Precisely." The last thing Rebecca wanted was attention from a married man. She braced herself and hoped he wouldn't do anything embarrassing.

CHAPTER 11

*N*ash watched as the scoundrel brewer handed Rebecca a tankard of ale and situated himself close to her side. His attention kept dipping to her breasts, which Nash knew from personal experience were most enticing. Nash wanted to jump up and pound the libertine into the ground.

"My lord, did you hear what I said?" asked the young lady next to him. Helen, whose last name he didn't even know to think of her appropriately, stared at him with her wide brown eyes. Her intention to gain his interest was utterly transparent, and Nash should have extricated himself from her presence long ago. She was not the sort of woman he would court.

Hadn't he decided not to court anyone?

Yet here he was in the company of three woman, flirting with them, while Rebecca, the only woman he really wanted to spend time with, was in the company of another man. A man who clearly wanted something improper, an affair perhaps. Except she was already having an affair with Nash.

What on earth was he doing away from her?

He was being his usual shallow self, engaging in harmless and mindless flirtation to keep deeper feel-

ings at bay. At least he recognized that he was behaving poorly—keeping Rebecca at arm's length
because she was getting too close. But did that matter
if he continued to be a boor?

After their eventful ride in the coach, he'd spent
all afternoon contemplating what to do. He tried
convincing himself that the tenet he'd introduced,
that whatever happens in the carriage stays in the
carriage, could mean anything that happened. So, not
only could they ignore the physical activities they'd
engaged in, they could also pretend as if their conversation had never occurred. They could go back to
the way things were. Before he'd told her anything
about Louisa. Before he'd allowed himself to be vulnerable.

But he hadn't even possessed the courage to discuss that with her. Any mention of Louisa or the way
he'd exposed his emotions made him incredibly agitated. Instead, he was doing what came easily, acting
as though he were a carefree roué who wasn't deeply
obsessed with the woman he'd grown to care about
over a very short period of time.

He started to shake and picked up his tankard
only to find it was empty. Why the hell hadn't that
blackguard brewer brought him a fresh tankard too?

Because he's not trying to find a way under your skirts.

"Excuse me, ladies," he said before he could even
comprehend what he meant to do.

He rose from the bench, wriggling out from between the two women on either side of him, and
smoothed his coat before striding to where Rebecca
stood with her sister and the degenerate brewer.

Nash smiled and hoped he didn't look like a feral
dog. "Barstow, I don't suppose you brought me an ale
as well?"

The scurrilous brewer frowned, his fair brows
forming a V. "I did not. We've plenty, though."

"Perhaps you could fetch it for me," Nash asked, knowing it was obnoxious of him to expect such a favor. "I'd go, but I promised Mrs. Sweet a promenade."

"In here?" The lascivious brewer laughed. "If you can take a promenade in the brewer's field, I'll give you an entire cask of my best ale!"

"I shall take that challenge," Nash said, offering Rebecca his arm.

She stared at him a moment, confusion in her gaze, then put her hand on his sleeve. Her touch nearly drove him to his knees. This had gone far beyond dangerous. He was facing utter disaster if he spent any more time with Rebecca.

But he didn't want to tear himself away from her. He'd tried tonight by focusing on the other women, but he kept looking for Rebecca, kept wishing she were part of the conversation, and kept cursing himself for being a coward.

Rebecca exchanged a look with her sister. "I'll find you and Phin shortly."

Leah nodded. "We need to leave to start the dancing in a bit."

Nash inclined his head toward Leah. "I look forward to speaking with your husband."

Then he moved Rebecca away through the press of people, realizing a promenade was nearly impossible. Still, he persevered. They would just move very, very slowly.

"Do you want my ale?" she asked. "I don't really wish for any more. It's rather strong."

"Yes, thank you." Nash took the tankard from her with his free hand and took a long drink.

"Thirsty?" she asked wryly.

"Trying to drown away the conversation of the past half hour." He grimaced. "That isn't kind of me to say. Miss...Helen is just extremely talkative."

"You seemed quite interested. Have you changed your mind about not looking for a wife?"

"No," he said quickly. "I—" He had no idea what he ought to say.

Action he could do—he wanted to bundle Rebecca into his arms and whisk her back to the inn, where he would strip her clothes away and drive her senseless with pleasure. Exactly what he'd done in the coach: push away his emotions in favor of something else to occupy his mind. And body.

Only, having Rebecca in his arms meant just as much as any emotion he might feel. Because it seemed his emotions were already entangled with her.

"What?" she prompted, looking at him expectantly.

He skirted a table pulling her along with him when a large man stumbled into them, breaking them apart. Cursing, Nash reached for Rebecca, but the man was in the way. Nash watched in horror as Rebecca fell, her head hitting the table before she landed on the ground.

"Bloody hell, mate!" someone shouted.

Nash hurried to Rebecca. She lay on the muddy ground, her face pale and her eyes closed. God, was she still breathing?

Panic froze Nash completely. He simply stood there, staring down at her, afraid to move.

Someone jostled him. "Creslow, what happened?"

Nash had no idea who had spoken to him. Then he saw two people kneeling down next to Rebecca. One was her sister. The other was her brother-in-law.

A buzzing sound, like a swarm of bees, filled Nash's ears. The world seemed to tilt sideways. What was happening?

Leah lifted her hand from beneath her sister's head. Her fingers were covered in blood.

Nash feared he was going to toss up his accounts. He spun away and came face-to-face with the towering beast who'd knocked Rebecca down. Another man was holding the beast's arm, his features angry as he tried to pull the beast away.

Without a word, Nash dropped the tankard and sent his fist into the beast's face. The man staggered backward, ultimately falling into another table as people scattered to move out of his path.

The buzzing faded, replaced by the cacophony of voices around him. Nash turned back to see Phin scooping Rebecca up in his arms. Her eyes were still closed. Her face still pale. Blood trailed down her temple and the side of her cheek.

Nash felt as though he was the one who'd been punched in the face. He could scarcely breathe. And nausea still threatened.

Leah was struggling to stand. Nash at least managed to move to help her up.

"Thank you." She stared at him. "You don't look well."

"Where is Phin taking her?"

"To Radford Grange. Someone's gone to find the doctor and send him there."

Nash didn't move. He didn't even breathe. He couldn't do either.

Leah started to turn. "Come along, one of the brewers is lending us his cart to transport her."

Somehow, Nash followed behind Leah. He didn't want to go. What if she was seriously injured? Or worse?

It wasn't a long walk to a side gate that had obviously been placed for the brewers to easily access the field. An unknown man helped Phin place Rebecca in the back of the cart.

Nash faltered, his step slowing. Fear gripped his insides and wrung him into a tight, excruciating knot. Phin helped Leah into the cart, then climbed in as the other man situated himself on the driver's seat.

"Come on, Nash!" Phin called.

Forcing himself to move, Nash hoisted himself into the back of the cart just before it started moving. He kept his gaze averted from Rebecca.

Leah sat beside him. "She'll be fine. I just know it."

Nash heard the concern in her voice. Was she trying to convince herself or him?

When they arrived at Radford Grange, the doctor was already there. Apparently, he'd been near the gate to the gardens and had been able to arrive quickly.

Phin climbed out of the cart and helped Leah down. Then he turned to Nash. "Help me pick Rebecca up."

Horrified, Nash froze. He didn't want to look at her, let alone touch her. The final days of Louisa's life flashed before him. She'd been so pale, gray even, and already lifeless. Dying had taken far too long and left him a shattered mess.

"Help me," Phin urged, prodding Nash into leaving the cart.

Together, they gently pulled Rebecca forward. Her head lolled to the side, and she moaned softly. She didn't open her eyes. Blood coated her neck.

"Can you take her?" Phin asked, his gaze moving to Nash's shaking hands.

Unable to speak, Nash shook his head.

"It's all right, I've got her." Phin swept her into his arms and hurried toward the house.

Leah met the doctor and guided him inside. Nash stared at the open door. It took him a moment to propel himself forward. All the emotion he worked to bury flooded him: terror, sadness, overwhelming grief.

He walked to the center of the entry hall, having no idea where to go.

"Would you care to wait in the drawing room?" the doddering butler asked.

"No." The word was dark and harsh. Nash didn't want to wait at all. He wanted to flee.

But he stood there, his body stiff as he worked to push down the emotions, back into the abyss from which they'd escaped. He had no idea how long he stood there, just that he'd finally entered some sort of numb state.

A maid came toward him, her expression kind. "Your lordship? I'm to tell you that Mrs. Sweet will recover. The doctor is preparing to stitch the wound now. You can come up, if you like."

She wasn't going to die.

Nash's legs nearly crumpled beneath him. He put his arms out to steady himself.

"My lord?" the maid said, her brow creased.

"I need to go," he croaked. "Please give Mrs. Sweet my best."

He turned and stumbled outside into the night that wasn't nearly as dark as the anguish inside him.

~

*R*ebecca's head felt as though someone had hit her with something very hard multiple times. And kept doing so. The throbbing was interminable.

She was currently propped up on several pillows —because the doctor had said she needed to keep her head elevated—in a very comfortable bed at Radford Grange. Phin had just left with the doctor, and Leah pressed a cool cloth to the side of Rebecca's head.

"Better?" Leah asked with a faint smile.

"Good enough."

"Do you want a few sips of tea?"

The doctor had said that Rebecca should refrain from eating or drinking until the morning, just in case she became ill. She hadn't yet and didn't even feel nauseated, despite the doctor asking her multiple times. He'd put three stitches in the side of her scalp. That had been the most excruciating thing Rebecca had ever endured. The doctor had allowed her a glass of whisky for that part, at least.

"I'd rather have more whisky."

"As it happens, there may be some in the tea."

Rebecca opened her eyes again and smiled at her sister. Then she winced. "Thank you, that would be lovely."

Leah got up from the bed and came back with the teacup. She held and tilted the cup while Rebecca slurped from the edge.

Setting the cup on the bedside table, Leah sat back down on the edge of the bed. "I'm so sorry this happened to you."

"I don't recall exactly what happened. I was walking with Nash, and then someone huge crashed into us. I remember falling, but not hitting my head." It seemed she might have lost consciousness for a moment or two, but Rebecca distinctly recalled lying on the ground amidst a crowd of people. "Where is he?"

"He was here, downstairs, but he left after he learned you would be all right."

He'd left her…again.

Leah frowned. "You look disappointed."

"I'm upset that he didn't stay." What was the point in hiding anything now? If there had ever been a point. "We were in the midst of a liaison. However, things began to fall apart earlier."

Leah gasped softly and pressed her finger to her lips. "Sorry, I'm just surprised."

"We actually met months ago when Aunt Jennet—Horatio's aunt with whom I've been living—brought me to a house party given by her friend, who happens to be Nash's cousin. During that meeting, we, er, had an...interlude."

"I will let my imagination make the most of that," Leah said with a smile.

"We weren't introduced. I knew who he was, of course, but he didn't know me at all. I didn't see him again until the other day, and he was shocked to learn his matchmaker was the woman from the library."

"An interlude in a library?" Leah giggled, then immediately sobered. "I'll stop interrupting."

"It's fine. There isn't much to tell. We met here in Marrywell, he told me of his requirements for marriage, we attempted to see if anyone at the festival would suit, he decided it was pointless to bother trying, given his requirements, and he dismissed me."

"The cad."

"I should perhaps include the part where he didn't wish to shag his employee, so he felt it best that I didn't work for him."

"Well, that puts things in a different light, doesn't it? Were you, ah, shagging before that happened?"

"No, I said we had to keep things professional, though it was difficult. I confess we seem to share a rather overwhelming attraction for one another."

Leah smiled. "That's nice." Then she frowned again. "Or would be if he hadn't run off."

"It doesn't matter," Rebecca said. "There was no hope for anything more than what we shared—a fleeting affair. Nash married for love and was heartbroken when his wife died. Hence, he refuses to fall in love again. I tried to marry for love, or at least the hope of it, and was heartbroken when Horatio turned out to be a selfish philanderer. Over the past few days, I've realized I would like to fall in love—for real this time." She took a steadying breath and willed her disappointment to fade. "I thought I might be falling for Nash. Which would have been bad. When you and I were talking in the brewer's field earlier, I'd decided I needed to end things with him."

Leah gently clasped Rebecca's hand. "Is that why you wanted to come and stay here?"

Rebecca nodded then immediately winced. "Dammit."

"You need to sleep," Leah said, sounding suddenly firm. "I've arranged for maids to sit and watch you all night—three of them will take varying shifts. We can talk about Nash in the morning. Or not. It's up to you."

"We don't need to." Rebecca wanted to put him out of her mind. "Will you send someone to fetch my things from the inn?"

"Of course. Phin and I will take care of everything. You just rest." Leah kissed Rebecca's cheek and stood. "I'll send the maid in. Sleep well."

"Good night." Rebecca watched her leave, then let her eyes flutter closed. This was a much better state for the persistent ache in her head.

What a perfectly horrible end to what had started as a lovely day.

The wound was bad enough, but knowing Nash had simply walked away without seeing her was more painful than she'd imagined. And why should it be? He'd promised her nothing, and any expectations she had were her own fault. Still, a friend—which he'd purported to be—would have ensured she was all right.

She turned her mind to the future. That was where her focus needed to be. She would recover and enjoy her time with her sister. Perhaps she'd even stay until the baby arrived. Rebecca looked forward to that, along with getting to know her other nephews and niece at Black Sheep Farm.

Then she would set about securing her next matchmaking client. Would Nash still write her a letter of recommendation? She wasn't sure she would ask. At the moment, it seemed a better idea to let their association fade away—like his presence tonight. If she was lucky enough to find love, it wasn't going to be with Nash.

CHAPTER 12

$\mathcal{T}$he ache in Rebecca's head was slightly less the following morning, but her mood was definitely worse. Sleeping had been difficult. Having a head injury was bad enough, but add in frustration over a certain gentleman, and Rebecca was grumpy.

She'd tried to focus on her future, on the plans she was making, but none of that solved her problem: she was already in love with Nash. And now she had to find a way to fall *out* of love. Preferably as soon as possible.

Unfortunately, she kept thinking of how hard that would be. In a very short time, she'd come to depend on him. He'd been there for her when she'd reconciled with Leah. In fact, he'd been instrumental in making it happen. Then, he'd provided wonderful support when she'd turned to Black Sheep Farm.

Until he'd abandoned her.

She knew why. Fear was a powerful motivator. It was why she'd jumped at the chance to wed Horatio and why she hadn't returned to Marrywell in nearly a decade.

The worst part was that instead of being furious with Nash for running off, she wanted to be there for him as he'd been for her. Even though she knew there was no point. He would never love her as she loved him.

Leah came into the bedroom with a bright smile. "You've a visitor!"

Rebecca's heart leapt.

Stepping farther into the room, Leah pivoted as the visitor came inside. It was their father.

Rebecca's heart turned to ash.

"Good morning, Becky Bex!" he said with a smile, brandishing a vase that held a bouquet of peonies. There were several shades of pink and even a white one.

"Good morning, Papa, but please don't call me that anymore."

Their father frowned. "Is it because Leah didn't have a nickname?"

"Yes." Rebecca sent her sister an apologetic glance.

"As it happens, he's now calling me Leah Leonie," Leah said, gently rolling her eyes, which their father couldn't see because of where she stood. Plus, he was looking at Rebecca.

Rebecca pressed her lips together lest she laugh. "Then I suppose it's fine. Perhaps we should all call you Papa Poppy."

He beamed. "I wouldn't be opposed."

Leah took the vase from him and brought them to the table next to Rebecca's bed. "Phin has gone to fetch your things from the inn," she murmured.

Though she didn't want to care, Rebecca would be desperate to hear how that went. Would Phin see Nash, or was it possible Nash had left? At last, she felt slightly nauseated, but it had nothing to do with her head.

"Will you let me know when he returns?" she asked softly, meeting Leah's gaze.

"What's this whispering?" their father asked,

moving to the other side of the bed, opposite where Leah stood.

"Nothing, Papa Poppy," Leah said. "I was just telling Rebecca that Phin has gone to the Buck and Maiden to retrieve her things since she'll be staying here."

"That's kind of him." He frowned, turning his attention to Rebecca. "Isn't your employer, Lord Creslow, at the inn? Why didn't he bring your belongings?"

Rebecca exhaled. "He's a marquess, and he doesn't have any retainers with him. You can't expect him to deliver my clothing and other items. Anyway, it may be that he's already returned to London." She was trying to prepare herself for the worst. Or, perhaps she was thinking the worst of him in an effort to fall out of love. Yes, that would work. Wouldn't it?

"Why would he leave while you're injured?" their father asked. "I had the impression he cared for you when he accompanied you to Black Sheep Farm yesterday."

Was that only yesterday? It seemed like a year ago. "Your impression was wrong," Rebecca winced as a pain sliced through her scalp. "Let us discuss something other than the marquess."

"Very well." Their father brightened. "How long will you be staying here at Radford Grange?"

"At least until I'm well." Which the doctor said would be about a fortnight, perhaps longer. Rebecca was in no hurry to return to Leighton Buzzard. Indeed, when she'd been able to turn her mind away from Nash, she'd considered her father's idea that she become the "Marrywell Matchmaker." She could provide assistance to a number of people during the festival and beyond.

"You are always welcome at my cottage at Black Sheep Farm," he said warmly, his eyes meeting hers.

"It would bring me great pleasure to be of support to you."

When Rebecca thought of returning to Marrywell permanently, living with her father had not come to mind. "Thank you for the kind offer, Papa Poppy. For now, I shall focus on resting and recuperating. I am also considering your suggestion about the 'Marrywell Matchmaker.'"

"What's this?" Leah asked with marked interest. "Does that mean you would live here in Marrywell?"

"It would. I'm still pondering the idea."

"I am delighted you would consider it!" their father said jovially. "To have you home along with Leah…" He looked between them, his eyes misting. "It's more than I ever dreamed."

Rebecca stared at him. "Why are you so pleasant now? Where was this side of you when we were children? When Mother was making all of us, especially Leah, miserable?" Asking those questions out loud was incredibly liberating.

Their father's face turned ashen, and he looked a little unsteady. Rebecca felt sympathy for him while also acknowledging that if he was suffering remorse, he deserved to.

"Because now I *can* be pleasant," he said quietly. "Harriet sucked all the joy from our lives. I'll tell you what I told Leah—I searched for, and found, love elsewhere. I loved Leah's mother very much. Her death nearly destroyed me. I worried for Leah not having a mother. I thought I was solving a problem when I brought Leah home, and I was relieved when Harriet agreed to care for her as part of our family."

The dull ache in Rebecca's head sharpened. "She never treated Leah like family."

"No, I suppose she didn't." He hung his head before pulling a chair to the side of the bed and sitting on the edge. Looking to Leah and then Rebecca, then fixing on a spot somewhere between them, he exhaled. "Harriet was indifferent to Leah at first. Later, when Leah was perhaps four or five, I began to notice that Harriet treated her a little more coolly than the rest of you. Honestly, she was such a prickly person, I didn't realize how bad she was for quite some time. I suppose I buried myself in managing the farm."

"I distinctly recall that, yes," Rebecca said.

"She wasn't always like that." A faint smile lifted his mouth. "She actually used to laugh, if you can believe it. Oh, she was never what you would call charming, but she was an excellent helpmeet, which my father said was the most important quality in a farmer's wife. Then, everything changed after she gave birth to Barn. She slowly became the frigid woman you all knew."

Rebecca could scarcely imagine their mother smiling, let alone laughing. She exchanged a wide-eyed look with Leah before frowning at their father. "I still don't understand how you endured her behavior and, more importantly, her treatment of us for so long."

"I suppose I felt I had to after asking her to take Leah in. I'd concluded her to be an unfeeling woman, but how could she be when she'd agreed to care for Leah? She even nursed her from her own breast."

"She had some feeling, then," Leah murmured. "Too bad it didn't last."

"No, it didn't. I can't begin to understand her or her behavior. After you were all gone, I stopped being kind. I stopped speaking to her almost entirely. Black Sheep Farm became a very quiet place, except when Barn and his family were in the house, which wasn't very often. I typically visited them at the cottage. Indeed, I suggested we swap residences a few years ago, but Harriet wouldn't hear of it." He looked to Leah, and his eyes were wet. "I can't thank you enough for paying her to leave. I don't deserve your kindness."

"My motives were selfish," Leah said wryly. "But I am glad that everyone else is pleased."

Their father wiped his hand across his eyes. "I'm just so dreadfully sorry about everything. If I could go back and change things, I would. I was such a coward. Fear can be a pernicious thing."

There was that word again—fear. Rebecca inhaled sharply, prompting Leah to look at her in question. But Rebecca said nothing, nor did she shake her head, for that would still be too painful.

Leah smoothed her hand over her growing belly. "What's important is how we go forward."

"We can't let fear direct us," Rebecca said.

"No, we cannot," their father agreed. "I hope we can all be happy. That's what I want most for both of you—and for Barn and Meg too." He gave them a hopeful smile.

"I'm certainly working on it," Leah said with a laugh, her hand still on her midsection.

Rebecca wished she were. But, at the moment, happiness seemed just out of reach.

～

Stretching open one eyelid, Nash glanced toward the bedside table where a half-empty bottle of port stood. He'd had to go in search of it after finishing the other bottle.

Nash's head pounded as a result of all the port, as well as the ale he'd consumed beforehand. But it had all been necessary. How else would he have found even a modicum of rest?

Only, he hadn't. While he'd closed his eyes and

succumbed to darkness, he didn't feel at all refreshed. Nor did he deserve to.

How was Rebecca this morning? Was she upset that he hadn't stayed to see her?

He was such a bloody coward.

But the thing he most feared had already happened. He cared about Rebecca. He was already suffering from the thought of something bad happening to her. Because something bad *had* happened.

The pain of seeing her lying on the ground, blood pooling from her wound, had completely incapacitated him. The agony of losing Louisa had returned tenfold. Would it never end?

A knock on the door to his chamber pulled him from his thoughts. He hadn't rung for anything, so what could it be?

Nash slid from the bed and donned his banyan. He moved slowly, in part due to his throbbing head, but also because of a sudden fear. What if it was bad news? Perhaps Rebecca wasn't fine after all.

"Nash? Are you in there? It's Phin."

Terror gripped Nash's chest. He stopped a few feet from the door and struggled to take quick breaths.

Another series of knocks. "Nash?"

Nash's heart bounced between his ribs as he opened the door and met Phin's gaze. "Morning."

Phin's jaw dropped. "Good Lord, you look awful."

"I feel awful." Nash clenched his free hand into a tight fist as anguish poured through him. "How is Rebecca? Please tell me she's all right."

"She is recovering. The doctor put three stitches in her scalp, so she's not feeling her best." Phin's brow creased. "May I come in?"

Nash unclenched his hand only for it to shake as a mix of relief and anxiety pulsed inside him. Instead of answering Phin, he opened the door wider in invitation.

Phin stepped into the sitting room. "I came to fetch Rebecca's things from her room. She'll be staying at Radford Grange while she recuperates."

"She really is going to recover?" Emotion shot up Nash's throat, and the last word came out dry and clipped.

"The doctor says so, yes. She passed a fitful night because of the pain, largely from the stitching. Leah was with her until late, but I made her go to bed. Since then, a rotation of maids have been supervising Rebecca to ensure she didn't take a turn for the worse." Phin fixed him with a dark stare. "It would have been helpful if you had come to sit with her."

Helpful? It would have been awful. Sitting by her bedside and watching to see if she got sicker. How many days and nights had he sat with Louisa? He'd watched her deteriorate, pieces of her dying a little every day, until she was finally gone. The doctor had thought that her invalidity would have prepared Nash for the loss. On the contrary, witnessing her transition from a young, vibrant woman to a sickly shell and ultimately a corpse had transformed Nash as well. He hadn't been ill, but he'd felt like nothing more than a bag of bones.

"I, ah, couldn't do that," Nash struggled to say. "It wouldn't have been appropriate," he added, somewhat lamely, at least in his opinion.

Phin's auburn eyebrows pitched into a sharp V. "Why not? It's my understanding that you and she have formed an attachment."

Rebecca had told them—her sister and Phin—that they were having an affair? Why *wouldn't* she confide in her sister? "It was temporary." That word sounded so cold to Nash now. He doubted anything about his association with Rebecca would be temporary. She would remain with him, in some way, forever. He met Phin's gaze. "Will you convey my best wishes to her on her recovery?"

"I can, but it would be best if you could do it yourself." Phin took an exasperated breath. "I realize we've only just met, but I must say that you're behaving like an ass. If nothing else, Rebecca was your employee. You could at least stop by Radford Grange for a short visit." He glowered at Nash. "Can't you?"

It took a moment and monumental effort for Nash to respond. "I don't know that I can," he whispered. The thought of seeing Rebecca lying in bed, her head bandaged... but she would be fine. It wasn't the same as Louisa. Still, he was shaking, "My wife... she died. She was sick for a very long time. I cared for her, stayed close to her bedside for months and months. Nothing I did mattered."

Phin came forward and gently set his hand on Nash's shoulder. "That sounds incredibly painful. I can see how that has affected you, that you are trying to avoid the pain of losing Rebecca in the same way. But she isn't going to die."

"Not today," Nash rasped. "I don't want this agony." But it was part of life, no matter how he tried to run from it. He thought of all the pain that Rebecca had endured, and still she carried on. In fact, she'd pushed through the pain of her past and even confronted it by returning to Marrywell and reconciling with her family. Unlike him, she didn't decry love or make foolish requirements in an effort to protect her heart.

There was another knock on the door, and Nash was grateful for the interruption. He moved around Phin and opened the door. Surprisingly, it was Rebecca's father.

Mr. Webster inclined his head. "Good morning, my lord. Sorry to bother you, but I'd like to speak with you for a few minutes, if I may?" He looked past Nash. "Phin, you're still here."

Nash's blood turned ice-cold. He gripped the side of the door as he regarded Webster. "Has something happened to Rebecca?"

Her father's brows gathered. "You address my daughter by her given name?"

"Er, yes. She was my matchmaker, after all."

"Hmmm." Mr. Webster came into the room and removed his hat, revealing his shock of mostly white hair.

Nash closed the door but didn't follow the man. "Is she all right?"

"Oh yes, she's quite well." Webster waved his hand as if that were a trivial question. "Besides the gash on her head, but she'll recover. I understand you witnessed the entire thing?"

"Yes."

"And did nothing to help my daughter." He flicked a glance at Phin, who said nothing, but looked at Nash expectantly.

They were going to be relentless. And why shouldn't they be? They loved Rebecca and wanted to see her well. Nash wanted that too.

He also couldn't deny what was now excruciatingly obvious despite his best intentions. He loved her. Desperately. If he didn't, the pain of nearly losing her would not be this great.

It seemed you could not completely wall off your heart, no matter how hard you worked at doing so. If Rebecca could face the pain of her past, why couldn't he? He'd already shown her the way.

"I was afraid," Nash whispered, looking down. "I still am. If I lose her the way I lost my wife…" His voice cracked on the last word. He clapped his hand to his mouth.

He felt another hand on his shoulder, but this

time, it was Webster. "I saw you with Rebecca yesterday at Black Sheep Farm. I know what it looks like when two people have an affinity for one another. Whatever is between you, it goes beyond matchmaker and employer." Webster squeezed Nash's shoulder, and Nash lifted his head. "I've spent too much time in my life keeping quiet and hoping for the best. I'm not doing that any longer, and neither should you. I have also lost a love, and you *will* recover. You can find happiness again. Indeed, you deserve to. Our time is too short to observe instead of *live.*"

His words hit Nash hard in the gut. He could live in fear, or he could live. He wanted to live.

He wanted to love.

"She must be terribly angry with me," Nash said quietly.

Phin cocked his head. "She's annoyed, but she'll understand if you talk to her."

"She will," Webster agreed. "I would be remiss if I didn't tell you that Rebecca hasn't had nearly enough love in her life. The thing she loved most was her pet goat, Marigold. The poor thing's mother died when she was very young, and Rebecca cared for her as if she were the creature's mother."

"What happened to Marigold?" Nash asked.

Webster grimaced. "She became ill when Rebecca was seventeen. Rebecca nursed the animal a few weeks until she passed peacefully."

Nash's gut clenched. Rebecca had suffered what he had. A goat might not be a person, but he would wager Rebecca had loved her just as much. He couldn't speak past the lump in his throat.

"Rebecca will be an excellent wife and mother—to the right man," Webster said. "She married poorly before, and it breaks my heart that I didn't see that."

Webster's words—that Rebecca hadn't had

enough love in her life—stuck with Nash. How could he deny her what she most deserved? If he loved her, and he did, shouldn't he shower her in it? Today, as soon as possible, and for all time?

He just needed to find the courage.

Nash wiped his hand over his face and regarded both men. "I'm not sure what to do. I've made an absolute hash of things."

"Clean yourself up, for one," Webster said. "Then get yourself to Radford Grange."

An idea began to form in Nash's mind. "Don't tell her I'm coming. I want to surprise her."

Phin fixed Nash with an expectant stare, as if he didn't quite trust him. "I hope it will be a good surprise."

"That is my intent." Nash hoped it would work.

CHAPTER 13

*A*fter a long nap, Rebecca woke in the afternoon feeling better than she had since hitting her head. The ache was less, and she was ravenous.

The doctor had visited before she'd gone to sleep and said she no longer required supervision. This was pleasing since Rebecca preferred to be alone to nurse her wounded heart.

She rang the bell that Leah had placed on her bedside table and waited for someone to come. While she didn't need anyone watching over her, she'd also been advised to remain abed until the following day.

Sitting up against the pillows, Rebecca closed her eyes and thought of what she might eat. She hoped she could have something more substantial than toast. A few minutes later, she heard the door creak open.

"Did you bring tea?" Rebecca asked.

When no one responded, she opened her eyes. And stared. Then her jaw dropped.

Nash stood at the foot of her bed, a tray in his hands. "Good afternoon, Rebecca." He smiled at her as if their last encounter hadn't ended with him dashing away into the night while she was having her head sutured.

While she was glad to see him—and relieved he hadn't left Marrywell—she was also irritated that he hadn't come sooner. "What took you so long?"

"I brought ginger cakes from the bakery," he said, waggling his eyebrows. As if that errand would have taken a good portion of the day.

She wasn't going to make this easy. He owed her an apology. "Your flirtations won't work on me. Anymore."

"What about delicious baked goods?" He gave her a hopeful look as he held out the tray.

Her stomach growled. "I'll have a ginger cake. Then you may explain yourself, or you may leave."

He came around to the side of the bed, moving with the grace of a cat and looking wonderfully handsome in a smart suit of blue superfine. His ivory waistcoat boasted a simple floral embroidery that was both masculine and elegant. He looked the complete opposite of how he'd dressed on the first day of the festival. What a silly enterprise that had been—as if he could ever appear unattractive.

Meanwhile, she had to look a fright after being forced to remain abed.

Setting the tray down on the table next to the bed, he whisked a serviette from his pocket and, with a flourish, laid it across her lap. He handed her a ginger cake, and their fingers touched as she took it from him.

Ignoring the jolt of pleasure his nearness aroused, Rebecca took a large bite of the cake.

"I was hoping I might speak with you," he said finally. "You don't have to talk, actually. You could just listen."

She watched him warily as she took another bite.

His brow was creased and his face a shade paler

than usual. He almost looked nervous. "I am so sorry about last night. I can't tell you how happy I am to see you sitting up and doing so well." He blinked several times, and she wondered if he was trying not to cry.

He was worse off than she'd thought. This went beyond fear. "I'm fine, Nash. Truly."

"I'm so relieved. I was so afraid. My fear froze me. Actually, it sent me to a rather dark, dismal place. It felt as though I was back with Louisa, my wife, before she finally died. I sat with her for months on end, watching her deteriorate."

His pain was so palpable. "I'm so sorry. Are you still there—in that dark place?" she asked softly, hating that he still suffered so much from his wife's death.

He shook his head. "Not anymore. And I have you to thank for that. You've shown me how to face the past. I just need to do it."

She itched to touch him, to comfort him. "I would help you, if you let me." Apparently, she wasn't ready to end their association.

He gave her a crooked smile that warmed her heart. "I was hoping you would say that. Can you for-give me, Rebecca? For leaving you last night and for not sharing myself with you as you've done with me. With each step you took toward healing and happi-ness with your family, I think my fear increased. I didn't think that could ever be possible for me."

"What couldn't be possible?"

"Allowing love again. Speaking of that, I've brought you something." With a twinkle in his eye, he swiftly turned from the bed and departed.

What could he have brought her that had to do with love? Her heart thudded as she waited for his return.

A moment later, he opened the door wide as he

carried a...baby goat into the bedchamber. Rebecca gasped and leaned forward from the pillows. "What are you doing?"

"I brought you a goat. You could call her Marigold if you like."

Tears stung Rebecca's eyes. This goat looked nothing like Marigold, who'd been white with a black stripe on her nose. This goat was reddish-brown with white socks. "How do you know about Marigold?"

"Your father told me."

Rebecca never would have expected that answer. "My father? When did you talk to him?"

"Earlier when he came to see me. He cares for you very much. It's rather heartwarming."

Her father had gone to see Nash? Why? While Rebecca wanted to know more about what had happened, she was too distracted by the adorable baby goat. "Where did you get her?"

"From Fieldstone. I went to see my friend, the Duke of Lawford. As it happened, they had a baby goat whose mother did not survive the birth."

"Poor baby." Rebecca pushed the coverlet back so she could get up.

"No, no. You aren't supposed to leave the bed." Nash hurried back to her and set the goat in her lap. The animal bleated and nuzzled her head against Rebecca.

Smiling, she stroked the goat's soft fur. "I can't call her Marigold. There was only one of her. But I could call her Ginger."

"Because of the color of her coat or the cakes?"

Rebecca laughed and immediately winced.

Nash touched her arm. "I'm sorry! I promise I won't make you laugh again."

She looked up at him. "Why are you doing all this?

I understand you feel bad. You apologized. There was no need to go to such lengths."

"There is every need," he said firmly. "Your father told me something else. That you have not had nearly enough love in your life. I would like to correct that egregious error."

Now she knew what he'd meant. Marigold had been her greatest love—so far. Breathless, she asked, "How will you do that?"

"By giving you all the love I have. My heart is apparently not as shriveled and black as I'd thought. I tried so very hard to guard myself from love, from the possibility of losing it again. But in the end, I was a massive failure." He was grinning in spite of his words.

She stifled her own smile. "You don't appear upset by that."

"On the contrary. I am happier than I have ever been. And I will be happier still if you perchance love me in return."

"You love me?"

"In ways I can't quantify or describe. You have rescued me from an abyss and showed me that my life is not over, that there is still much to do and experience. I'd like to do it with you, if you'd have me."

"Is that a…proposal?" Rebecca could scarcely believe his revelations.

He dropped to his knees beside the bed. "It is. Be my wife. Please. Every moment I spend with you is filled with joy and hope. I haven't felt those things for a very long time. I hope, in time, you'll perhaps love me too. I will spend the rest of our lives—however long that may be—demonstrating my devotion. I will never, ever abandon you again."

"I already love you. That is why I wanted to end our affair. I didn't see the point in continuing when I knew you couldn't love me in return."

He took her hand and brought it to his mouth, pressing a long kiss to her palm. "I was such an arse. Can you ever forgive me?"

"I can. I do. And I will marry you." She watched as his lips spread in a wide smile and his eyes glowed with emotion—love, she now knew. What a marvelous thing this was to share love with another person. Rebecca felt glorious and bright, like the sun.

Nash kissed her hand again. "You have made me the happiest of men. I adore you." He stood and leaned down to press his lips to hers. The kiss was sweet and full of delicious promise.

Rebecca stroked Ginger, whose eyes had closed as she laid her head on Rebecca's knee. "Why did you bring me a goat?" She knew why, but wanted to hear him say it.

"Because you loved Marigold, and you lost her. I loved my wife—so very much—and I lost her too. I can't replace her, just as you can't replace Marigold, but I can start anew."

And he said it in a far lovelier manner than she'd expected. She looked up at him. "I want you to share the joys—and sorrows—of your time with your former wife. Can you do that?"

He nodded. "I will."

"Kiss me again before you fetch me a pot of tea. And more food. The cakes were delicious, but I require something a bit more substantial, if you please."

He bent his head and touched his lips to hers. "Your every wish is my greatest desire." He kissed her before looking down at Ginger. "What of your new pet?"

"Leave her be. She is the most wonderful gift." Rebecca met his gaze and basked in the love she saw there.

"No, you are."

"*Love* is," Rebecca said, never more sure of anything in her life.

~

Fifteen days later, Nash married the second love of his life. He'd just managed to have the first banns read the very day he'd proposed, rushing to the Marrywell church for the evening service.

After a lovely wedding ceremony at the same church, Nash escorted his beautiful wife into the drawing room at Radford Grange. They were greeted with a rousing chorus of "Huzzah" from the many guests who'd insisted on attending that morning's wedding service.

Nash looked over at Rebecca and could scarcely believe how vastly and quickly his life had changed. Not even three weeks ago, he was preparing to meet his matchmaker. He could never have imagined her or anything that had happened next.

And he was so bloody grateful. To have found Rebecca. That she had recovered from her injury so well. That he had managed to be vulnerable and allow himself to love again—and to be loved.

The first to greet them was Rebecca's father. Monty Webster had shed a tear or two as he'd given his daughter to Nash at the altar. Nash had already thanked the man for talking sense into him, but did so again that morning in a soft whisper.

"You look absolutely radiant, my dear Becky Bex!" Webster said with a proud smile.

"Thank you, Papa Poppy." Rebecca moved on to the next guest, her sister Meg, who'd come from Salisbury with her husband and three children. They embraced briefly, and Meg tried to smooth a curl that had come loose behind Rebecca's ear. However, the errant lock was stubborn and refused to remain where she'd placed it.

"I tried," Meg said with a sigh. "Your hair was always impossible to tame."

Nash loved it. Though he had yet to loosen the red mass and fan it across a pillow, he intended to that very night. They'd spent the last fortnight apart, despite Nash lodging at Radford Grange, while Rebecca had recuperated.

Nash kissed Meg's cheek. She was slightly taller than her sisters, and her hair was a few shades darker than Rebecca's—more auburn than red. "I'm so glad you could come," he said.

"Make my sister happy, please." She gave him a saucy smile, and he promised he would.

After shaking Meg's husband's hand, he caught up to Rebecca, who was speaking with Nash's mother. Georgianna Nash, the dowager Marchioness of Creslow, had arrived a few days earlier, eager to meet her new daughter-in-law. Just as Nash didn't think he could be any happier, they had formed an instant bond.

He hugged his mother, then they moved on to his sisters and their husbands, who'd also come to Marrywell for the wedding. That his family had enthusiastically gathered around him as he wed a second time meant more than he could say.

Their friends, the Duke and Duchess of Lawford, and Rebecca's "Aunt" Jennet rounded out the guests for the wedding breakfast. Lawford asked Rebecca how Ginger was faring.

"She's quite happy here. I hope she won't mind coming to London." Rebecca glanced toward Nash. He'd agreed they should bring their pet with them to London for the remainder of the Season and then to Creslow Manor, where they would go after.

Nash pushed that from his mind. The idea of

taking Rebecca there—the place where Louisa had lain ill and died—filled him with dread, but he was ready to face the past, even if he wasn't looking forward to it.

"You're taking Ginger to London?" Sadie, the Duchess of Lawford, asked.

Rebecca shrugged. "She's my pet."

Sadie smiled. "I think that's lovely."

Glancing toward their host, Nash whispered, "Phin will be glad to preserve what remains of his peonies."

Sadie's eyes rounded as she laughed softly. "Oh dear."

"Apparently, they are quite tasty," Rebecca said, her eyes twinkling.

Nash stared at her a moment, still not believing that she was his and he was hers.

Phin approached them, and Nash wondered if he'd heard what they'd said. He didn't appear to, as he simply informed them that breakfast would be served momentarily.

As Rebecca continued speaking with Sadie and Law, Nash's mother came up beside him. She seemed to want to talk to him, so he turned toward her, stepping slightly away from the others.

"I don't want to interrupt, my dear Benji." She was the only person in the world who called him that, and it never failed to make him feel like a small, cherished boy.

He smiled at her. "You aren't. I'm so glad you're here."

Her blue eyes sparkled with love. "I wouldn't be anywhere else. Your Rebecca is so lovely. I'm so delighted to see you so happy. I worried you wouldn't ever be again."

"I worried that too," he said quietly. "But, I am fortunate to have met Rebecca."

"You have been lucky twice. To have loved two people who loved you greatly in return is a blessing."

He couldn't help but think of her misfortune—loving his father only to have him be unfaithful, even while he'd claimed to love her. "Mama, perhaps you should come to the matchmaking festival next year. You may also find love."

She laughed brightly, then gave him a coy look. "I don't think that will be necessary."

Nash froze for a moment, hopeful. "What do you mean by that?"

"You recall Mr. Davenport?" she asked, referring to a widower who lived around the corner from her in Bath. He was about the same age as Nash's mother, and they'd been friends for several years.

"Of course. He always beats me at chess."

"Does he?" She smiled prettily, as one does when they are thinking of someone whom they hold in affection.

"Mama, have you and Mr. Davenport formed an attachment?"

"We may have." Her brow creased slightly. "You don't think I'm being foolish? Surely, we're too old to start anew."

They were only in their middle fifties, but even if they'd been twice that, he would say the same thing. "One is never too old for love, and we should pursue it and grasp it and hold it tightly whenever it crosses our path." He took her hand, squeezing it gently. "I couldn't be more glad for you. And Mr. Davenport. Do tell him I'll be ensuring he makes you happy."

"Oh, he does, my dear boy. He absolutely does."

Nash hugged her tightly. "This is the best wedding gift I could have asked for."

～

*T*hat evening, Nash and Rebecca lay together in his former bedchamber at the Buck and Maiden. They'd wanted to spend their first night together alone, or at least away from Radford Grange.

Returning to the room where they'd finished what they'd started months earlier had seemed fitting as they started their married life. After Nash had demonstrated just how very much he'd missed her, he held her close and asked if she was feeling all right.

"I'm fine," Rebecca said with a touch of exasperation. "You were very gentle with me, which is a bit of a shame, but I suppose we have a lifetime for you to demonstrate your passion in other ways."

He nibbled on her earlobe. "Count on it." The word "lifetime" sent an icy jolt through him, but he was learning to set his fear aside. He meant to enjoy every day with Rebecca and look to their shared future without anxiety.

"Do you think Ginger is all right?" she asked.

They'd allowed their nephews and nieces to take her back to Black Sheep Farm while they were staying at the inn. "I'm confident she is well cared for. I do think Abigail might be bedding down with her in the barn tonight."

At age nine, Barbara was Meg's eldest child. She'd been absolutely besotted with Ginger. So much so that Meg had said she anticipated there would be goats in their future.

Rebecca chuckled. "You may be right."

Nash stroked her hair, which he'd managed to arrange across the pillow, a bright array of shining red against snow white. "Oh, I meant to tell you something wonderful."

"That you love me?" she teased.

He kissed her nose. "Yes, that. Always. Also, my

mother seems to have also found love again with her dear friend and neighbor, Mr. Davenport. He's a delightful gentleman. I look forward to introducing you. We'll need to plan a visit to Bath."

"Goodness, we have very busy days ahead," she said. "I'm so delighted for your mother. Perhaps we'll have another wedding this year."

"That would be lovely. What of your father?" Nash asked. "Do you think he would try to find love again?"

Rebecca turned her head toward him and laughed. "Are you trying to become a matchmaker now?"

Grinning, he shrugged. "I suppose I just want everyone to have what I do—an everlasting love with a person who makes me feel whole."

She turned toward him, her expression turning serious. "Do you really? Feel whole, that is."

"I do." He caressed her cheek. "You are my heart and soul, my dearest love."

Her lips curved into a beautiful, seductive smile as she cupped his head and brought her mouth to his. "And *you* are mine."

EPILOGUE

*W*hile last year's matchmaking festival had seemed plagued with rain, this year's was so far warm and sunny, and today, the day of the Grand Picnic, was the finest yet. Rebecca sat in a chair on one of the blankets because she was too heavy with child to maneuver herself to the ground, or, perhaps more importantly, to easily get back up.

Nash fluttered about like a lost bee, desperate to be busy and helpful, but not sure how he could do that. He'd already fetched Rebecca's chair, a small table on which he'd placed lemonade and a fan in case she became too warm. She'd used the latter to wave him off, telling him to visit the brewer's field with Law, Phin, and Barn.

Except none of them had left their cluster of blankets.

Barn's children ran about while Sadie's oldest, who was now two, toddled after them. There were babies too—Barn and Thea's youngest and Leah's daughter, who had just started to crawl. It was no wonder Phin hadn't gone to the brewer's field. He and Leah were occupied with ensuring Rose didn't make her way off the blankets.

Sadie came and sat next to Rebecca. She was also

expecting a child, though not until September while Rebecca was due to give birth next month. When Law had seen Nash bring Rebecca a chair, he'd done the same for his wife.

"How are you managing?" Sadie asked her with a smile. "I found the last month or so almost unbearable. I just felt so *large.*"

Rebecca kept most of her thoughts and feelings to herself because Nash was already agitated about the coming birth. He was terrified of losing Rebecca or the child, and she wouldn't contribute to his anxiety. "Don't tell Nash, but I am uncomfortable. I only sleep an hour or two at most at a time. I confess I am not looking forward to the next few weeks. Is it bad that I wouldn't mind if the babe came early?"

"Not at all. And if you don't mind my saying so, you do look as though you could be ready soon."

Rebecca laughed. "Leah and Thea have said the same thing—not in front of Nash. They've both asked if I have the dates right, but I absolutely do."

A sharp pain in Rebecca's back made her shift in the chair. She reached for the fan as perspiration rose along the back of her neck.

Sadie's brow creased. "Are you all right? That was quite a wince."

"Just a back pain. I've had them off and on all day." Rebecca unfurled the fan and moved it in front of her face. "I told you I was uncomfortable."

"All day?" Sadie's eyes rounded. "It may be that the babe would like to come early too."

"But it's my back that hurts," Rebecca said, feeling slightly alarmed. As much as she wanted relief from carrying, she wasn't quite ready. "Perhaps I just need to take a walk." She stood from the chair and felt a rush of liquid on her thighs.

She promptly sat back down.

And stood back up again as soon as she realized there would be a wet mark on her backside.

"Sadie, I need to go to Radford Grange."

Sadie rose quickly, her eyes widening. She grabbed Rebecca's hand. "Right away. What's happened?"

"I'm not sure, but I think the baby does want to be early. When things become wet—" She didn't have to finish before Sadie nodded sharply and knowingly.

"Yes, the baby wants to come early. Let's get you to Radford Grange." Sadie put her arm around Rebecca and guided her toward where the men were seated.

Nash looked up immediately, his brows leaping together. "What's wrong?" He scrambled to his feet before Rebecca could answer because another pain gripped her back. Then it moved around her, squeezing her from back to front.

Gasping, Rebecca reached for him. "It's time to have a baby."

He grasped her hand, his face going pale. "We need to get you to Radford Grange."

Nash had insisted on taking his coach, which was parked outside the nearest gate to the gardens. He swept her into his arms and hurried in that direction.

"We'll meet you there!" Sadie called after them.

Rebecca clutched at his neck. "You can't carry me all that way!"

"The hell I can't." He increased his pace and was panting desperately by the time they reached the coach.

After depositing her on the seat, he instructed the coachman, Timmons, to make haste. When he joined her in the coach, she could see how stricken he was by this sudden development.

"I'm fine, my love," she said soothingly. "All will be well."

"Yes," he murmured, his gaze fixed on her swollen belly. "But it's too soon." He lifted his eyes to hers, and in them, she saw panic. "It's too soon."

"It's not that soon. It may be that your son just didn't need as much time as other babies. Both Leah and Sadie have commented on my size and asked if I could possibly have estimated the date wrong."

"Could you?" He sounded both hopeful and anguished.

"I suppose it's possible," she lied. She was certain as to when she'd had her last courses.

His face fell, alarming her. "I didn't tell anyone to fetch the doctor."

"They will, along with Mrs. Campion." Sadie's stepmother, who'd just married her father last summer, had helped to deliver many babies, including Leah's daughter.

Rebecca took her husband's hand and squeezed. "Everything is going to be just *fine*. I need you to believe that." She met his gaze, and though he hesitated, he ultimately nodded.

Just as another pain wrapped around Rebecca's midsection. She sucked in a breath, then swore as the coach hit a rut.

"Careful!" Nash shouted, as if there were anything the coachman could do about the quality of the road.

"Breathe, Rebecca," Nash said, sounding surprisingly calm. He kept hold of her hand and put his other hand behind her back, where he stroked her in large, round circles, his palm skimming over her back.

At last, the pain subsided. Rebecca knew that the closer they came, the sooner the babe would arrive. "Are we nearly there?"

"Just turning up the drive," Nash said. "You'll be tucked up in bed in no time." He smiled, and she leaned over to press a kiss to his cheek. "Thank you."

As soon as the coach stopped, Nash threw open the door and leaped down. Rebecca eased herself off the seat and Nash helped her out. Her feet didn't touch the ground as he picked her up once more and carried her to the house.

Timmons rushed to open the door. Waiting for the incredibly slow butler was not an option. "Fetch Mrs. Appleton," Nash called to the coachman, referring to the housekeeper.

"On my way!" Timmons responded before dashing off.

"I can walk," Rebecca said. "You can't carry me up the stairs."

"I can and I will." He made it to the landing. "All right, you can walk the rest of the way. With my help." He gave her a stern look as he set her down.

Rebecca found her footing and frowned at him. "You're very commanding. And not in the delightful way you are in bed on occasion."

He closed his eyes briefly and smiled—that brilliant, handsome smile that never failed to make her knees weak. But in this moment, she wasn't sure if that was due to the smile or another pain rippling across her back to her abdomen.

"A moment," she said, gritting her teeth and dropping her head forward as she clasped his arm and squeezed while the contraction passed.

"Whenever you are ready," he said, again sounding remarkably calm. "You're doing wonderfully."

Rebecca lifted her head and glowered at him. "How would you know?"

"Law and Phin said this might happen."

"What?" Rebecca began to breathe more easily as the pain lessened. "I'm ready."

Nash helped her up the staircase. "Hold the railing with your other hand, please."

"What did Law and Phin say might happen?"

"That your mood would, ah, sour. And that you may become particularly…upset with me."

"I see." Neither Leah nor Sadie had mentioned that. "I do know that they were tossed from the room before the babes came. But you aren't doing that." Rebecca looked over at him as they reached the first floor. "You're staying so you can see that everything is fine."

And so that if anything *did* happen, he would be there with her.

Thankfully, nothing did. Except for the surprising number of babies.

~

*R*ebecca was exhausted but triumphant. She'd given birth not once, but *twice*. Her daughter and son were small, but the doctor had proclaimed them wonderfully healthy. He'd also congratulated Rebecca on her fine work and thanked Mrs. Campion for her assistance.

The latter was still there, fussing about the room and currently trying to usher out everyone who'd come to see the babies.

"Yes, we all need to go," Sadie agreed. She came and kissed Rebecca's forehead before looking at the babies, who were snuggled together sleeping in the cradle next to the bed. "I'm so very happy for you all," she whispered.

She tugged on Law's arm as she rounded the bed toward the door. Law stifled a yawn and went to clap Nash, who stood beside the cradle, on the shoulder. "Good luck with sleeping." The duke chuckled before leaving with his wife.

Phin lingered on the other side of the bed while Leah came around to take Rebecca's hand. "I know this isn't what you planned, but I'm so pleased you had the babies here. Not just with me. But in Marry-well. Home."

"I didn't think of it as home for a long time," Rebecca said. "And I'm not sure I do now. Home is wherever he is." She shot Nash a look and wasn't surprised to see him gazing at her with open adoration.

"And them," Nash said, inclining his head toward their children.

Children.

Rebecca had never imagined there would be two.

"Yes, definitely them," Rebecca agreed.

Leah kissed Rebecca's cheek. "Try to sleep. One of the maids will check in periodically to see if you need anything. I'll see you in the morning."

"Indeed, you already are," Phin said, nodding toward the window, where the light of dawn was easing around and between the curtains.

Leah laughed. "Goodness, time has no meaning during birth." She walked back around the bed, and she and Phin left.

Mrs. Campion was the only person remaining. She came to the bed, her brown eyes bright against her dark brown skin. "I'm going to speak with the maids about how best to help you. I'll be about for a couple of hours then I'll return later today to see if you need any help with feeding."

Rebecca wasn't sure she wanted to voice her concern—or any concern—in front of Nash, but then he beat her to it.

Nash stepped toward the bed and looked to Mrs. Campion. "Will she be able to feed them both?"

"She shouldn't have any trouble. We women are made to do this, and we are stronger than anyone can imagine, especially men." She laughed softly and patted his arm. "You were exceptional and most help-ful. You'll be an excellent father."

"I hope so."

"Both of you should sleep if you can." Mrs. Campion walked back to the other side of the room where she picked up a small pile of the remaining soiled linens. "I'll join Law in wishing you luck. My best advice to you is to sleep when they sleep these first weeks."

Then she was gone, and Rebecca was alone with Nash and their babies. She yawned, suddenly desperate to close her eyes. Finding sleep had ceased to be a problem for her, with the exception of the last few weeks. As soon as she'd married Nash and shared his bed, her troubles with slumber had vanished. She was certain it was due to his remedy—the one he'd recommended the night they'd met at Clipstone Hedge.

"Why are you smiling like that?" he asked.

"I was thinking how I used to have difficulty sleeping. When we met, you suggested bed sport might help."

He laughed. "I did, didn't I? What a saucy rake I was."

Rebecca yawned again. "All that talk of sleep has made me want to do just that."

"You should," he said softly, sitting down next to her on the edge of the bed. "I'm going to stare at them awhile longer." His warm, loving gaze settled on the cradle.

A surge of love so strong that it nearly made her gasp rushed through Rebecca. "I still can't believe there are two of them."

Nash turned his attention back to her, his eyes rounding briefly. "When the doctor said he thought there was another, I was sure I'd misheard him."

Their daughter, Matilda, had arrived first. Mrs. Campion had been tidying her up when Rebecca had said she was still feeling sharp pain. It was nearly a half hour later that their son, Marcus, had decided to join them, which meant they had different birthdays.

"You nearly swooned," Rebecca said. "I'm glad Leah was here to attend you while you gathered your wits."

"Honestly, I'm not sure I found them all," he said with a sheepish smile. "Perhaps I will tomorrow."

Rebecca smiled. "You see, I told you everything would be fine."

"You were only a little wrong."

She cocked her head to the side. "How is that?"

"Fine doesn't begin to describe it." He leaned toward her, his mouth hovering over hers. "I believe the correct word is *perfect*."

Thank you so much for reading **Matching the Marquess**. I hope you enjoyed it! Catch up with the first two books in the **Marrywell Brides** series, **Beguiling the Duke** and **Romancing the Heiress**!

And don't miss Erica Ridley's linked series set in Marrywell, Heart & Soul. Catch up with **Chasing the Bride**: Professional fixer Hudson is meant to find his aristocratic employer's runaway bride and bring her back to the altar—not to accept her indecent proposal... and fall in love with her himself!

Would you like to know when my next book is available and to hear about sales and deals? Sign up for my VIP newsletter, follow me on social media:

Facebook: https://facebook.com/DarcyBurkeFans
Instagram at darcyburkeauthor
Pinterest at darcyburkewrite

And follow me on Bookbub to receive updates on pre-orders, new releases, and deals!

Need more Regency romance? Check out my other historical series:

Rogue Rules

When a young lady is ruined, her friends vow none of them will ever be ensnared by a scoundrel again. They will resist every gentleman's charms even—and especially—if it means gaining a reputation for being impossible to woo. It will take extraordinary rogues to break their rules...

The Phoenix Club

Society's most exclusive invitation...

Welcome to the Phoenix Club, where London's most audacious, disreputable, and intriguing ladies and gentlemen find scandal, redemption, and second chances.

Matchmaking Chronicles

The course of true love never runs smooth. Sometimes a little matchmaking is required. When couples meet at a house party, provocative flirtation, secret rendezvous, and falling in love abound!

The Untouchables

Swoon over twelve of Society's most eligible and elusive bachelor peers and the bluestockings, wallflowers, and outcasts who bring them to their knees!

The Untouchables: The Spitfire Society

Meet the smart, independent women who've decided they don't need Society's rules, their families' expectations, or, most importantly, a husband. But just because they don't need a man doesn't mean they might not *want* one...

The Untouchables: The Pretenders

Set in the captivating world of The Untouchables, follow the saga of a trio of siblings who excel at being something they're not. Can a dauntless Bow Street Runner, a devastated viscount, and a disillusioned Society miss unravel their secrets?

Wicked Dukes Club

Six books written by me and my BFF, NYT Bestselling Author Erica Ridley. Meet the unforgettable men of London's most notorious tavern, The Wicked Duke. Seductively handsome, with charm and wit to spare, one night with these rakes and rogues will never be enough...

Love is All Around

Heartwarming Regency-set retellings of classic Christmas stories (written after the Regency!) featuring a cozy village, three siblings, and the best gift of all: love.

Secrets and Scandals

Six epic stories set in London's glittering ballrooms and England's lush countryside.

Legendary Rogues

Five intrepid heroines and adventurous heroes embark on exciting quests across the Georgian Highlands and Regency England and Wales!

If you like contemporary romance, I hope you'll check out my **Ribbon Ridge** series available from

Avon Impulse, and the continuation of Ribbon Ridge in **So Hot**.

I hope you'll consider leaving a review at your favorite online vendor or networking site!

I appreciate my readers so much. Thank you, thank you, *thank you*.

ALSO BY DARCY BURKE

Historical Romance

Marrywell Brides
Beguiling the Duke
Romancing the Heiress
Matching the Marquess

Rogue Rules
If the Duke Dares
Because the Baron Broods
As the Earl Likes
When the Viscount Seduces

The Phoenix Club
Improper
Impassioned
Intolerable
Indecent
Impossible
Irresistible
Impeccable
Insatiable

Matchmaking Chronicles
The Rigid Duke
The Bachelor Earl (also prequel to *The Untouchables*)
The Runaway Viscount
The Make-Believe Widow

One Night for Seduction by Erica Ridley

One Night of Surrender by Darcy Burke

One Night of Passion by Erica Ridley

One Night of Scandal by Darcy Burke

One Night to Remember by Erica Ridley

One Night of Temptation by Darcy Burke

Secrets and Scandals

Her Wicked Ways

His Wicked Heart

To Seduce a Scoundrel

To Love a Thief (a novella)

Never Love a Scoundrel

Scoundrel Ever After

Legendary Rogues

The Legend of a Rogue (prequel available only to newsletter subscribers)

Lady of Desire

Romancing the Earl

Lord of Fortune

Captivating the Scoundrel

Contemporary Romance

Ribbon Ridge

Where the Heart Is (a prequel novella)

Only in My Dreams

Yours to Hold

When Love Happens

The Idea of You

When We Kiss

You're Still the One

Ribbon Ridge: So Hot

So Good

So Right

So Wrong

Prefer to read in German, French, or Italian? Check out my website for foreign language editions!

ABOUT THE AUTHOR

Darcy Burke is the USA Today Bestselling Author of sexy, emotional historical and contemporary romance. Darcy wrote her first book at age 11, a happily ever after about a swan addicted to magic and the female swan who loved him, with exceedingly poor illustrations. Join her <u>Reader Club newsletter</u> for the latest updates from Darcy.

A native Oregonian, Darcy lives on the edge of wine country with her guitar-strumming husband, artist daughter, and imaginative son who will almost certainly out-write her one day (that may be tomorrow). They're a crazy cat family with two Bengal cats, a small, fame-seeking cat named after a fruit, an older rescue Maine Coon with attitude to spare, an adorable former stray who wandered onto their deck and into their hearts, and two bonded boys who used to belong to (separate) neighbors but chose them instead. You can find Darcy at a winery, in her comfy writing chair balancing her laptop and a cat or three, folding laundry (which she loves), or binge-watching TV with the family. Her happy places are Disneyland, Labor Day weekend at the Gorge, Denmark, and anywhere in the UK—so long as her family is there too. Visit Darcy online at <u>www.darcyburke.com</u> and follow her on social media.

facebook.com/DarcyBurkeFans

x.com/darcyburke

instagram.com/darcyburkeauthor

pinterest.com/darcyburkewrites

goodreads.com/darcyburke

bookbub.com/authors/darcy-burke

amazon.com/author/darcyburke